"The reader is riveted to the words, the action."
— *Robert Ludlum*

"Block's grasp of character is extraordinarily honest...his combining of the genre requirements has an expert touch."
— *Philadelphia Inquirer*

"Everything mystery readers love best."
— *Denver Post*

"If Lawrence Block writes it, I read it."
— *Mike Lupica*

"Marvelous...will hold readers gaga with suspense."
— *New York Newsday*

"A superior storyteller."
— *San Antonio Express-News*

"A smooth, chilling suspense novel that stretches nerves wire-tight before they snap."
— *Boston Herald*

"Block knows how to pace a story and tighten the noose of suspense. He writes sharp dialogue and knows his mean streets."
— *San Francisco Examiner*

"He is simply the best at what he does...If you haven't read him before, you've wasted a lot of time. Begin now."
— *Mostly Murder*

She called me at the Stennett. It was around noon and I was asleep when the phone rang. I yawned, lit a cigarette, answered it.

"You're a son of a bitch, Nat," Anne said.

I laughed softly.

"A real son of a bitch. Why didn't you have a few goons come over and beat me up? Or something subtle, like acid in the face?"

"I like your face."

"Uh-huh. All of a sudden I don't have a job. All of a sudden I don't have a roof over my head. All of a sudden I can't even buy a drink in this goddamned town. Isn't that cute?"

I dragged on my cigarette. "It sounds rough."

"Doesn't it? You don't issue invitations, Nat. You issue ultimatums. I don't like ultimatums."

I didn't say anything. I smoked my cigarette and let her dangle on her end of the phone.

"No place to live, no job, nothing to do. What am I supposed to do, Nat?"

"You should leave town."

"Should I?"

"Sure. You should come to Las Vegas. With me."

A pause. "An ultimatum, Nat?"

"Call it an invitation..."

Sinner
MAN

by **Lawrence Block**

A HARD CASE CRIME NOVEL

A HARD CASE CRIME BOOK
(HCC-126)
First Hard Case Crime edition: November 2016

Published by

Titan Books
A division of Titan Publishing Group Ltd
144 Southwark Street
London SE1 0UP

in collaboration with Winterfall LLC

This book is a work of fiction. Names, characters, places, and incidents either are the products of the author's imagination or are used fictitiously, and any resemblance to actual events or persons, living or dead, is entirely coincidental.

Paperback edition ISBN 978-1-78565-001-7
Hardcover edition ISBN 978-1-78565-134-2
E-book ISBN 978-1-78565-002-4

Design direction by Max Phillips
www.maxphillips.net

Typeset by Swordsmith Productions

Printed in the United States of America

Visit us on the web at www.HardCaseCrime.com

SINNER MAN

I

"Oh, for Christ's sake," I said. "You can get up now. No matter how long you lie there, nobody's gonna give you a fucking Academy Award for it."

No response. I noted the trickle of blood from her temple, the angle of her head where it met the surround of the field-stone fireplace.

I stood there, waiting for someone to run the film backward, waiting for her to rise up from the carpet, waiting for my hand to draw back from her face, to delete the blow that had sent her stumbling and falling and cracking her head on the stone with a sound that still echoed through the room.

Waiting for the past five minutes to erase themselves.

I don't know how long it took for me to kneel down next to her. I felt for a pulse that wasn't there, tried to remember what else you were supposed to do. In movies they'd see if there was a trace of breath to fog a pocket mirror, but strangely enough I didn't happen to have a mirror in my pocket.

There was a large mirror mounted above the fireplace. I thought of hauling Ellen to her feet and pressing her face against the mirror, but that didn't strike me as a very good idea. Or I could try smashing the thing and holding a piece of it to her lips, but I had the feeling I was already in for enough bad luck, I didn't need seven years more.

I could just wait a few hours and see if she cooled to room temperature. That would be a pretty good sign, wouldn't it?

Not that I needed a sign.

What I needed was someone to blame.

How about Ray Danton? Or Legs Diamond, the slick fellow

I'd watched him play a few hours earlier? Or another slick fellow, Johnnie Walker by name, whose picture was on the bottle on the mantel over the fireplace. The bottle was half empty or half full, depending on whether you were an optimist or a pessimist.

But there looked to be two bottles, one the mirror's reflection of the other. One was half empty, I decided, and the other was half full.

I dismissed the bottle in the mirror and uncapped the real one.

Haven't you had enough to drink?

Ellen's voice, clear as a bell in my head, as if it were still echoing around the room. God knows she'd spoken the sentence often enough over the years, and the answer was always no, I hadn't had enough to drink, now that she mentioned it.

But maybe this time she was right. I'd need a clear head, wouldn't I?

For what?

I compromised by taking a short pull straight from the bottle, then recapped it and set it down.

My wife was dead. And while I might try to blame her—for provoking the blow, for falling clumsily, for landing wrong—it was clearly my fault and not hers. Nor could I blame those three old smoothies, Ray and Legs and Johnnie.

Though they'd all played their parts...

It's hard to say where anything starts, but it may have been that day at lunch, and it wasn't Johnnie Walker but his cousin Gordon who supplied the jigger in the woodpile. Gordon's Gin, that is to say, and when my lunch companion suggested a second round of martinis, I thought it sounded like a good idea.

After lunch we went our separate ways, and my way was

supposed to lead to an appointment with a client. I'd been soft-ening the guy up for a while now, and he was just about ready to bite on a hefty straight life policy, and all I had to do was meet with him and reel him in.

That second martini loosened me up just enough to question the need to waste the afternoon in that fashion.

Not that it was an afternoon that made one rush to the beach, or hike in the mountains. It was a gray day, constantly threatening to rain but never quite getting around to it. A day to sit in a movie house and watch something dark and nasty.

I was in my car, driving in the direction of my afternoon appointment. And I caught a red light at the corner of Wayland and Lamonica, and I looked over to my left at a movie mar-quee. *The Rise and Fall of Legs Diamond*, I read.

I'd read something about the film. It had just opened. And I knew a little about Legs Diamond, who'd operated in New York and up the Hudson Valley to Albany, which is not that far away from Danbury.

And I've always loved gangster movies.

I parked the car, checked the schedule, discovered that the picture was going to start in twenty minutes. That gave me just enough time to find a pay phone and cancel my appointment, and find a liquor store and switch from Gordon to cousin Johnnie. Just a half pint, to keep me company while I watched Ray Danton bring the late Jack "Legs" Diamond back to life.

For a while at least, until a hail of bullets cut him down.

I watched the film through to the end, and when it was over I wished it was the first half of a double feature. But there was just the one picture, and I walked out thinking that maybe that was just as well, because I'd sipped my way through the half pint of scotch while Legs was occupied with rising and falling.

I suppose I was a little bit drunk. Closer, certainly, to drunkenness than to sobriety. But I didn't feel drunk. I felt deeply relaxed, very comfortable within my own skin, and at the same time I felt energized, ready for something to happen.

Yeah, right.

I sat in the car, left my key unturned in the ignition, and gave myself over to the film I'd just seen. Somewhere in there, buried beneath the drama and action, there looked to be a moral. And, because that's how Hollywood works, it pretty much had to be *Crime Does Not Pay*.

And I suppose it didn't, if you went by the ending. Legs Diamond wound up dead.

But doesn't everybody? All of us, even those of us who wear Brooks Brothers suits and sell whole life, wind up the same way.

But Legs sure had fun while it lasted…

I stopped at a liquor store on the way home, and my house was empty when I walked in the door. I cracked the seal on the bottle—Johnnie Walker Red Label, a fifth of the same medicine I'd had a half pint of in the tenth row at Loews Danbury. I used a glass, and when it was empty I filled it up again, and when it was full I sipped at it until it needed filling.

Somewhere along the way Ellen came home.

I don't remember how the argument started, or what it was about. The fact that I'd been drinking was mentioned, you can be sure of that, and that line—*Haven't you had enough to drink?*— was spoken, and answered silently, unless you count the sound of liquor transferred from bottle to glass.

She put dinner on the table, though neither of us had much of an appetite for it. And then the argument resumed, and she said something about the folly of breaking appointments with valuable clients, and I said something about having to see movies during the daytime, because I could no more stomach the Rock Hudson–Doris Day crap she liked than she could sit through a good gangster movie. And it got nasty, the way an argument can, and that's what you get in a marriage that's not very good and probably never should have happened in the first place.

But that would have been nothing new, an argument, with each of us saying things we shouldn't have said, and me drinking too much, and in the morning we'd pretend it hadn't happened.

Nothing we couldn't live with.

Except her mouth just wouldn't quit, and I reached for the scotch bottle, and she said it was already half-empty. I could have said that was a pessimistic way of looking at it, that you could as easily say it was half-full, but that sort of banter wouldn't have matched my mood. I had hold of it by the neck, and her eyes widened as I stepped toward her, bottle raised overhead.

She thought I was going to hit her with the bottle. But I swear that was never in my mind, it was enough that the threat cut off the flow of words. I set the bottle down.

And the words started flowing again.

And, finally, I gave her a smack. Openhanded, across the face, just to make her shut up.

Nothing that hadn't happened a couple of times before.

Except she fell, and don't ask me why because I didn't hit her all that hard. And she landed wrong.

And now she was dead.

Did they still have the death penalty in Connecticut? I couldn't remember.

It seemed to me there'd been a movement to abolish it, but I didn't know if it got anywhere. I smoked a cigarette and thought about it. I remembered the bullets that Legs Diamond got, and

I wondered how the state did it. A chair wired for electricity? A rope around your neck? A room full of gas?

Or just a lifetime in a prison cell?

Whether or not there was a death penalty, I didn't have to worry about it. Not even a low-grade moron would plan to murder his wife by smashing her head in their own living room. There were plenty of rational ways to kill Ellen, and I'd had fantasies of most of them at one time or another, running them through my mind the way you do. Some were simple and some were elaborate, but none of them was anything like what had just happened.

So I had not committed premeditated murder. What would a jury call it? Second-degree murder at worst, temporary insanity at best, with some kind of manslaughter in the middle, and the most likely.

So I wouldn't get the chair, or the rope, or gas, or life—whatever was dispensed in this state. I'd catch either a short-to-middling prison sentence or an acquittal. All I had to do was pick up the telephone and call the local police and inform them that I, Donald Barshter, had just accidentally killed my wife. They would do the rest. From that point on it would be out of my hands, a judicial tug of war between the district attorney's office and my own lawyer. I could relax and let them figure out what they were going to do to me.

I reached for the phone, I held the receiver to my ear with my left hand and fitted my index finger into the little hole marked O for Operator. Then I took a deep breath.

And stopped cold. And took my index finger out of O for Operator and put the receiver back in the cradle.

This picture came to me. It was a picture of my little world with everything gone right—an acquittal, say, or the suspended sentence they give you that says you're a solid citizen who made a mistake and please don't do it again. I wondered how many people would be likely to buy an insurance policy from Donald Barshter, wife-killer. I wondered how many of the friends Ellen and I had shared would ask me over for a few drinks and a rubber or two of bridge. I thought about the way the good folks of the town would stare at me on the streets and the way the mothers would chain their daughters home when I was walking around.

I thought of courtrooms, jails and newspaper photos. I thought of all the little details that completed the picture. All I had to do was call the police and I would make that picture my life.

But what was the alternative? Ellen looked up at me with a flat empty stare. She was dead, I had killed her—and the dumbest cop in town could figure out that much with his eyes shut. I couldn't get Ellen's blood out of the carpet, couldn't patch her head with plastic wood. I was her husband and that made me suspect number one from the start. No matter how cute an alibi I cooked up, the police would pick it to pieces and laugh in my face.

So I reached for the phone again. And stopped.

Donald Barshter, thirty-two-year-old representative for one of the country's leading life insurance companies, was a goner. The life he had been living for those thirty-two years was over. He was finished, washed up, through.

Well, to hell with him. I still had a chance.

It was Friday night. In a little less than half an hour it would be midnight. Ellen had been dead almost an hour. Her skin was already growing cold. I still sat on the edge of our bed. I was working my way through the last cigarette from the pack.

I had picked a bad night to kill her. There was the unimpressive sum of fifty-three dollars in my wallet and a few bucks in change in various pockets here and there—which was not nearly enough.

I got rid of the cigarette, went to my desk and began adding up assets with paper and pencil. There was fourteen hundred in the checking account, thirty-five hundred in the savings account. There was the cash surrender value of a few life policies, a couple thousand tied up in stocks, a little more in mutual funds. But there was no time to surrender the insurance and no time to sell the securities. I had forty-nine hundred dollars in cash assets and I couldn't get to them until Monday morning.

Since the banks opened at nine, I had fifty-seven hours to kill. Fifty-seven hours to spend at home with Ellen, who was dead.

I went downstairs and made myself a cup of instant coffee. I found a fresh pack of cigarettes and smoked one while I drank the coffee. Then I came back upstairs and returned to the bedroom. I picked up Ellen's body and carried her to her closet. She was heavy but not hard to carry. I placed her on the closet floor and closed the door on her. The room was much emptier without her body in the middle of the floor. It also made her death that much less real. And thinking that much easier.

Fifty-seven hours. The daytime hours would be the hard ones, with the phone ringing and the doorbell ringing and too many people to talk with, too many explanations to invent. Nights would be easier.

And, because there was nothing else to do for the time being, I got into my own bed and slept. There was a lot of tossing and turning before sleep came. There were hectic dreams later, but when I awoke I couldn't remember them.

There were two phone calls for Ellen Saturday morning and one during the afternoon. I told three women that she was out, that I didn't know when she'd be back, that I'd have her call them. I made one call on my own. We were supposed to have dinner with three other couples Saturday night, after which we were scheduled to play bridge at somebody's house and spend a dull evening with them. I called Grace Dallman and told her we wouldn't be able to make it, that an aunt of Ellen's in North Carolina had died and that Ellen was catching a train that evening for Charlotte. The funeral would be held Monday and she wanted to get there early.

It was a handy story. Ellen actually did have an aunt in North Carolina, a noisy and unpleasant woman who had never been sick a day in her life as far as I knew. But I liked the story and stuck to it that evening when a few more of Ellen's friends called up. I told them all that she would be back Tuesday or Wednesday. They were all properly sympathetic.

So I spent Saturday night watching television and nursing a can or two of beer. I have no idea what I watched on the twenty-one-inch silver screen. It was a way to pass time and nothing more. For the time being I wanted to do as little thinking or planning as I possibly could. That would come later when my mind was a little looser and the fact of Ellen's death a little further removed from reality. Any thinking now would be colored too strongly by fear, shot through too thoroughly by worry. There was time.

I went to sleep at two, with the fifty-seven hours pared to thirty-one. I slept until ten and cut the time down to twenty-three hours. We were getting right down to the wire.

I scrambled a pair of eggs and fried bacon for Sunday breakfast. I smoked the day's first cigarette with coffee and thought about one thing I'd been consciously avoiding. Now it was time to think about it.

Because the killing of Ellen wasn't manslaughter anymore. The killing wasn't manslaughter and it wasn't second-degree murder—it had ceased to be either the minute I stuffed Ellen's corpse in her closet and decided to leave her to heaven. Now it was Murder One, the big one, and I was a murderer in the first and foremost degree.

The killing had stopped being manslaughter the minute I decided not to call the police, the minute I decided not to go to court or to jail. I couldn't plead for gentle justice anymore. I couldn't get caught at all.

So now I was the man on the run. The fact that I wasn't running at all, that in fact I was having breakfast in my own kitchen, had nothing to do with it. I had to run—hell, I had to do more than that. A lifetime on the run was nothing but a life sentence to a mobile jail.

I had to be someone else. I had to be someone who was not Donald Barshter, someone who didn't live in this town, someone who didn't sell insurance. Someone who hadn't murdered his wife. Someone who wasn't running.

Someone with a new name and a new address and a new personality. Someone with his own life to live and his own fish to fry. Someone settled in his own little groove.

And it couldn't help being an infinitely better groove than selling insurance to people who didn't really want or need insurance; living with a woman I didn't even like, let alone love; making monthly deposits in the savings account and the checking account and balancing these precariously with monthly payments on the house and the car and the television set and the washer and the dryer; and saying the same dismal words day after day to the same dismal people.

The impersonation might even be fun. Like an actor playing a part. Like Danton playing Legs.

I left the breakfast dishes in the sink and wondered if anybody would ever wash them and dry them and put them to bed in the proper cupboards. I went upstairs again, took a shower and got dressed. I found a good leather suitcase of mine, one of the few that hadn't been monogrammed. I opened it, propped it up on the bed and looked through drawers and closets for things to put in it. I found few things. It was going to be necessary to travel light. The wardrobe that suited Donald Barshter would not suit the man I was going to become.

Clothes are part of a personality. Donald Barshter's tweeds and pinstripes and regimental ties and button-down shirts were part and parcel of his grownup Ivy League personality—they went hand in hand with the briefcase and the actuarial tables and the memo books. Barshter's clothes wouldn't do.

I packed three white shirts, a few pairs of undershorts and T-shirts, a few of my louder ties. I didn't bother with suits or shoes—I would wear one suit and one pair of shoes and that would be enough. The less of Donald Barshter's clothes I had, the less I'd have to get rid of later on.

That more or less took care of Sunday. During the afternoon I wandered around the corner to the drugstore and picked up a copy of the *New York Times*. I ran into a few people I knew and mentioned that Ellen was out of town and that I was living a bachelor's life for the next day or two. I even set up an appointment to talk a fellow into carrying more life insurance. Then I went home and alternated between the *Times* and the television set until it was time to go to sleep.

I didn't sleep much.

I had the alarm set for eight-thirty but I was up before it had a chance to go off. I was completely awake the second I opened my eyes and my blood nearly sang with energy. I showered and shaved and dressed, picking out an anonymously gray suit and a pair of Italian shoes. I tried to remember the last time I'd felt so thoroughly alive, so excited and ready to go. I couldn't remember a comparable morning in years. There had been similar mornings in Korea, of course, and a few in the first years of marriage. But since then excitement had not been part of my life, had not been a common feeling at all. Which was a shame—excitement is a healthy thing.

I tucked my wallet in one pocket, my keys in another. I scooped up a handful of loose change and dropped it into a third pocket. Next I found my bankbook and my checkbook and made room for them. I picked up the suitcase, which wasn't heavy at all, and carried it out of the house to the car. I put the suitcase in the back of the car on the floor.

The two banks where I had accounts were across the street from one another on Chambers. I cashed a check for thirteen hundred at the bank where I had my checking account, leaving a hundred dollars to keep the account warm. I crossed the street and emptied the savings account, explaining that I had a cash deal pending and needed the dough in a hurry. The teller told me I could take a low-interest loan and keep my account intact but I managed to talk him out of it. I left the bank with forty-eight hundred-dollar bills in my wallet. I hoped the sum would be enough.

Now I felt tension building up in my body like steam in a teakettle just before it whistles. I crossed the street to my car, the morning sun coming down strong. I couldn't help feeling that everybody was looking at me, that I was marvelously conspicuous with Cain's mark on my forehead. Or maybe there was a special mark for uxoricide, a particular sign for wife-killers.

I got into the car and drove out of town. There was a perfectly good railroad terminal in town just a few blocks away— but I had to go somewhere safe, to a place where I wouldn't be stepping on acquaintances. I drove to Hartford and put the car in a downtown parking lot. I carried the suitcase to the railroad station. On the way I shredded the parking check and dropped it in a trash can.

It was a shame to give up the car but I could hardly keep it. And it might have hurt more if I had liked the car or if it had been paid for. As it was I owed an impressive sum to the finance company, so it wasn't quite as though I were abandoning the entire car. Just the power steering and the power brakes and the automatic transmission—I could live without them just as I could live without Ellen.

There was a line in front of the ticket window in the railroad station. I stood in line and waited my turn, still feeling painfully conspicuous, still feeling that everyone was taking careful notice of me. Finally I was at the front of the line. I bought a ticket to New York and went to the platform to wait for my train. It came and I boarded it.

2

I went as far as Syracuse and took another train out of there at six-fourteen P.M. and headed west. Nathaniel Crowley sat alone in a seat in the coach nearest the dining car. At Syracuse he had bought a hat, a black fedora with a very short brim, now resting on top of a folded New York tabloid on the seat next to him. His legs were crossed at the knee and his hands rested easily in his lap.

But he wasn't as relaxed as he looked. His nerves were stretched taut and his heart was beating a little faster than it usually did. His mind refused to rest. It planned, plotted, schemed and came up with ideas and rejected them. His mind worked a mile a minute, more than could be said for the train— which crawled.

I'm not projecting. I know precisely how Nathaniel Crowley felt. I was Crowley. Nathaniel Crowley—a new name to take the place of Donald Barshter, to fit the new personality and the new life. The name had to be nationless because a handle like Giardello or Rabinowitz or Pilsudski would only get in my way. But the name had to be a little more memorable than Joe Jones or John Smith—it had to be something simple but with a certain amount of individuality.

Thus Nathaniel Crowley, Nat for short. It had come to me somewhere in the course of the void between Albany and Utica, and when it came I didn't fight it. I let it run through my head a few times and decided that I liked the sound of it. Nat Crowley. It had a nice, easy, breezy ring to it. Easy to spell, easy to pronounce, easy to remember. Probably easy enough to scrawl on a hotel register in Buffalo.

Buffalo. Because that was where Nat Crowley was going to live. For a variety of reasons, some of which might be worth thinking about.

You see, I had to live somewhere. And the place I picked had to be big enough so that a new face in town wouldn't stick out like the proverbial sore thumb. That consideration knocked out all the towns with less than half a million inhabitants.

Size was the first requirement but there were others. Location was a prime one. If I picked a town in a state in the South or West, my accent was going to work against me. I could never create a good niche for myself in Mississippi, for example, because I'd always be that Yankee who talks funny.

Another big thing—I had to pick a city where I wouldn't run into anybody I knew. That killed New York, where I knew far too many people, where I could never feel altogether safe. The same consideration killed Los Angeles and Chicago and Philadelphia and St. Louis and Detroit, because those cities booked too many conventions.

By the time I had finished ruling out city after city for one reason or another, Buffalo headed the list and seemed to fill the bill. Its population was just shy of a million. And the only visitors the town ever had were Canadians who didn't know any better. Which was fine with me.

Now it was a few minutes after six. We were supposed to hit Buffalo a little after midnight.

I got up from my seat, leaving the newspaper and the hat for the time being. I walked to the diner, sat down at an empty table and ordered rye with soda and a rare steak. I drank the rye and ate the dinner and wondered if anybody had come across Ellen's body yet. It didn't seem likely. Unless I picked up a little bad luck somewhere along the line, I had two or three days of grace before some buffoon opened the wrong closet door and screamed for the police.

By that time Nat Crowley would have a life of his own. He would be in Buffalo. He would have a new wardrobe and a new apartment and a start on assembling a new circle of friends. He would also have a new job.

His employer would be the local crime syndicate.

I finished my dinner, had another drink and smoked a cigarette. I left the diner and went back to my coach. I sat down, looked at my tabloid for a minute or two, then folded it again and thought some more about Nat Crowley. He was going to be a criminal. Not a wife-murderer, like Donald Barshter. A professional criminal, the kind that doesn't go to jail.

There were reasons for this. I had to earn a living, since the five grand I was carrying wouldn't last forever. And I couldn't walk into the nearest insurance agency and tell them to hire me. I could invent Crowley easily enough but it was something else entirely to invent a past for him. I couldn't outfit Nat with employers' references and past job summaries and the rest. A respectable employer would run a check just as a matter of course and pretty soon the police would come knocking on my door. Then it would all be over with.

So Crowley couldn't work for anybody who would check on him. That left him with two choices—he could go into business for himself, using whatever remained of his five grand as operating capital, or he could get some sort of tie-up with the kind of boys who don't ask to see your references. Like the syndicate, or the Mafia, or the organization, or the combination, or the outfit, or the mob—or whatever term the press is using these days to conceal its overwhelming ignorance of the whole thing.

I couldn't think of a business offhand that I felt competent to run or that I could pick up with the amount of capital I could afford to invest. That left me with the mob. And there was another reason for the mob, as far as that went. It fit in with the new personality I was inventing for Nat Crowley.

Because the personality would be as much of a disguise as Crowley would have. Crowley would be six feet tall, with brown eyes and mud-colored hair and properly unobtrusive features. In short, he would look exactly like Donald Barshter. I could play all kinds of games—dyeing my hair, wearing platform shoes, paying a plastic surgeon to twist my nose around. But if I did any of those, one day or another the chosen disguise would slip and some clown would figure out that it was a disguise and that therefore I was hiding something. Which was all I needed.

There are better ways to disguise yourself. You leave your hair its usual color and keep it the usual distance from the ground. Your face remains the same. You change what's behind it.

You change the clothes from the quiet tweeds and pinstripes and flannels to suits with more of a flair. You buy longer jackets and spend more money on them. You buy expensive shoes and noisy ties. You wear a hat—it alters the shape of your face at least as thoroughly as a nose job and at the same time the hat changes the tone of your appearance tremendously.

Little things. Nat Crowley would walk less hurriedly and more confidently. His voice would be lower, but not so much lower that it would be a strain. He'd speak slowly and he'd hold the words to a minimum.

More little things. Barshter drank either scotch on the rocks or dry martinis. Crowley would drink rye and soda or a bottle of premium beer. Barshter played lousy golf and listened inattentively to classical music. Crowley would hang out at jazz clubs and stick to spectator sports. He might catch the Friday fights from ringside or spend an afternoon at the track but you'd never catch him out at the country club for a weekend in the pool.

It wasn't just a matter of props. Because props are something you use in an act and this had to be more than an act—it had to be real. I had to let myself slip into Crowley's personality, playing it by ear at the beginning, living with it until it became my own. Eventually I would be Nat Crowley. I would live his life and think his thoughts and see the world through his eyes.

I could do worse, a lot worse. By now I was looking forward to the whole masquerade the way a satyr with a virgin bride looks forward to his wedding night. Donald Barshter had shot his wad years ago. There was nothing left for him—no kicks, no excitement, no sense of being alive—which, indirectly, was why Ellen and I had fought so much lately. We had nothing better to do. More directly, that was why I had knocked her around during a rare moment of passion. And why I was riding the train to the little city of Buffalo.

Crowley's life wouldn't be dull. He wouldn't waste his days selling insurance and he wouldn't come home each night to a boring wife who, when she bothered to talk to him at all, would babble on and on about slip covers for the living-room chairs and similar stimulating domestic topics.

Halfway to Rochester I stood up and walked to the john. While I was there I locked myself in the can and went through my wallet. There were a few traces of Barshter along with all that money and I wanted to get rid of them. I tore up a slew of membership cards in a variety of organizations, a driver's license, a Social Security card, a withholding statement, a batch of business cards—mine and others'—a fishing license, somebody's telephone number and similar trivia. I tore up all my credit cards, wishing I had had the time to run up some bills I would never have to pay. But you can't have everything.

I flushed all this garbage down the toilet and left it on the tracks for the gandy dancers to puzzle over. I took a long look at myself in the mirror, first with my glasses on, then without them. I'd picked up the glasses years ago for reading; somewhere in the course of time I'd started wearing them permanently. Now it was a slight strain without them. I figured I could get used to it.

The window gave me a hard time. You'd think they'd leave the john windows open full-time. They don't. This one was stuck and I had to wrestle to get it open. I pitched the glasses into the middle of New York State and closed the window again. A face looks different without glasses. But that wasn't the only reason I gave them the heave.

You see, Nat Crowley wouldn't wear glasses. He'd squint first.

We were only a few minutes behind schedule getting into Buffalo, which was better than I had expected. I wrestled my suitcase from the rack overhead, put on my hat and left my newspaper on the train. I went into the terminal, looked up hotels in the Yellow Pages and decided that the Malmsly seemed about right. As far as I could figure it, it was the city's second-best hotel. I found a taxi and rode to it. I tipped the cabby, surrendered my suitcase to a bellhop and signed the register as Nat Crowley, Miami. The bellhop took me upstairs to a large and comfortable room. I gave him a dollar and got rid of him.

I turned on the TV set, saw a comedy show strictly for squares and then watched a newscast. There was nothing very significant on the news. A stock I owned had gone up quite a few points but this didn't do me any good now. I turned off the TV, undressed and washed off the smell of the train in the shower.

Then I called the desk and had them send up a kid to take care of my suit. The same bellhop appeared a few minutes later, took my suit and a second dollar and told me it would be cleaned and pressed by morning. That was good, because it was the only suit I had.

3

I was awakened the next morning by a discreet knocking on my door. I rolled over and looked at the ceiling for a minute or two, finding my bearings and reminding myself just who I was and where I was. Then I wrapped myself up in a towel and opened the door. It was the bellhop—a different one this time—with my suit, cleaned and pressed and much better to look at than it had been after so many hours on the train. I gave the bellhop a dollar and closed the door again.

Bellhops were becoming expensive. They'd cost me three dollars so far and ordinarily I would have given them a quarter each. But Nat Crowley had to be a big tipper. His personality was costing me money.

I dressed and floated downstairs in the elevator. I had corned-beef hash with a poached egg on it in the wood-paneled Men's Grill. Then I walked outside to have a look at downtown Buffalo. A fairly stiff wind blew smoke and soot at me. A scattering of morning shoppers crossed Main Street against the light and looked generally unhappy.

I walked along Main Street. I passed what seemed to be the main department stores. I passed half a dozen movie houses, none of them open yet. I passed a shop that sold ties for fifty cents each, a shop offering souvenirs of Niagara Falls and exploding cigars and magic tricks and Japanese transistor radios, a shop where any suit in the store was twenty dollars and any jacket fifteen. I passed bars, some with music and some without, some expensive and some cheap, all of them rather empty now.

I smoked a cigarette all the way down and pitched the butt into the gutter. There were plenty of others there to keep it company.

But I had no complaints. While there was little to see, I wasn't a sightseer.

I went into a bank and talked to a clerical type about opening a regular checking account. I handed him four thousand dollars and a trio of phony Miami business references. I was fairly certain he wouldn't bother checking them out—hell, I was opening an account, not applying for a loan. When a man hands you cash you don't ask him his religion.

I left with a dead-fish handshake and a bright little checkbook, something temporary until they had time to run off some imprinted checks for me. Then I stopped off at the five-and-dime and picked up a few packs of cheap stationery. I dashed off a batch of idiot letters, addressed them to Nat Crowley at the Hotel Malmsly and sent them scuttling off to a half-dozen mailing services throughout the country. In return for two bits a letter, these outfits would mail my letters back to me. It was a cheap and happily simple way to establish a background.

In a drab building a few blocks from the hotel I applied for a Social Security card. I didn't need any identification for that since the card itself isn't supposed to be used for identification. A girl with thick eyeglasses gave me the card and I stuck it into my wallet. The next stop was the Bureau of Motor Vehicles where I picked up a blank for a driver's license. The license section was part of the application, so I took the whole business to the library where I rented a typewriter and filled out the license part. Then, back in my hotel room, I forged the stamp with a ballpoint pen. This wouldn't do for driving but I wasn't planning on driving anywhere. The license made fine identification.

Other things could come later. Like the Diners Club, library card—all the little pasteboard certificates that tell the world who you are. I'd pick them up when the time came.

That afternoon I stopped in a men's shop and bought a wardrobe. I bought two suits—a pearl-gray sharkskin and a black mohair. I bought shirts and socks and shoes. I bought ties—they didn't exactly glow in the dark but they said hello firmly. I paid the clerk in cash and told him to send everything to me at the Malmsly when he had a chance.

Dinner was a plate of spaghetti and meatballs washed down with a couple glasses of sour red wine in a small Italian restaurant a block off the main stem. I followed it up with two cups of strong black coffee and went through the evening paper. I skipped the national and international tripe and tried to get impressions of the city from the local news. I found out what I wanted to know. There was a good amount of petty crime and plenty of organized gambling. It looked as though I wouldn't have much trouble finding the fellows I was looking for. They had a lot of things going.

I left the restaurant, wandered back to Main Street and dropped into an innocuous bar where I had a rye and soda. I was beginning to develop a taste for the drink. And I was also beginning to develop a feel for the sort of part I was playing. After a day of being Crowley I didn't have to ask myself quite so often how Nat Crowley would react to a situation. I simply reacted that way.

Still, it was hard to tell whether my new personality was working. So far there had been no test.

I walked around for a while but there wasn't a hell of a lot to look at. It was Tuesday night in downtown Buffalo and the shoppers had all gone home. The strip joints weren't ready for action yet and the whores wouldn't start whoring for another three or four hours. I went to a movie and killed time watching cowboys chase Indians. By the time I left the theater things had changed. The strippers were stripping and the whores were getting ready to whore.

I took another long walk along Main Street. I headed uptown, gave a wino a quarter to get rid of him, shook my head no at a streetwalker before she had a chance to ask. I turned west and stepped into another bar. I felt it was time for a test. The first test.

It was an ordinary bar. It wasn't the mob's fine and private place—I hadn't come across that bar yet—nor was it a neighborhood affair where you went to grab a beer and watch television and get away from your wife. It was a run-of-the-mill downtown ginnery. Two ancient hustlers held up one end of the bar and two equally ancient lushes weighted down the other end. The bartender was fat and ugly. The jukebox blared forth rock-'n'-roll. A Canadian, judging by his accent as he called for a drink, stood alone at the bar with a few men on either side of him. I managed to get next to the Canadian and order rye and soda. I paid for the drink with a twenty and let my change stay on top of the bar.

I studied the Canadian. He was about my age but he wasn't wearing it too well. He looked just about drunk enough and miserable enough to be belligerent. I hoped he was.

I poured the rye into the soda and sloshed them around with a swizzle stick. I took an exploratory sip and then put the drink back on the bar. I took out a pack of cigarettes, shook one loose, put it in my mouth and set it on fire.

Then I spilled the drink all over the Canadian.

He was one unhappy Canadian. He took a quick step back, then took a sad look downward at the damage. His jacket was wet, his pants were wet, his shirt was wet. His tie was ready for the ashcan. He studied all this and then raised his eyes to meet mine.

"Sorry," I said. I motioned to the bartender and told him to bring us each a fresh drink.

"Spilled your goddamned drink all over me," the Canadian said.

"An accident. They happen."

"All over me. Soaked to the skin. I ought to punch you in the nose, you son of a bitch."

I gave him a hard look. "I said it was an accident, baby. Don't lean on your luck."

"Dirty bastard."

I told him to shut up.

The bartender came over and set fresh drinks in front of both of us. I mixed mine again and wondered where the Canadian would take it from here. It was his move. He could push it or leave it alone. I hoped he would push it.

He did. "Dirty son of a bitch," he said again. And when I turned around to look at him he tried to slug me.

It was a mistake. He sent me a telegram first, then wound up and threw what was supposed to be his Sunday punch. It was Tuesday and he missed. I brushed the fist aside with my left hand and swatted him with the right. He gagged and stepped back. Then he lowered his head and came in again.

I hit him in the chest, over the heart, hard. I chopped a short right to the underside of his jaw and he straightened up. I kicked him in the pit of the stomach and he fell forward on his face.

He lay there and made little noises without moving. I walked over next to him, looked at him for a moment and gave him a very short and very hard kick in the side of the head. It was hard enough to knock him out but not hard enough to kill him. His eyes closed and he stopped making his little noises.

The jukebox was the only noise in the bar. It went on making bad music while everybody else clammed up and tried not to look at me. They didn't manage it.

I picked up the bills, leaving the change for the barkeep. I motioned him over and he came to me, his eyes wary.

"I don't want trouble, Mac."

My eyes smiled gently. "No trouble," I said. I peeled a single off the top of the roll of bills and handed it to him. "For him," I said, pointing to the Canadian on the floor. "I spilled a drink on him. This is so he can get his suit cleaned."

I turned and walked out of the bar.

I had been in a combat unit in Korea. It all happened years ago but parts of the experience had been sharp, raw, vital. Those parts were still clear now. Some of them came back to me now and then, sometimes in dreams, sometimes when I was lost in thought.

Now I remembered the first time I'd seen combat. Most of Korea was nothing much more than too much cold and too much mud and too many corpses. The first day of fighting was memorable.

Not the action itself. The action had something to do with a hill—we were trying to hold it, or to take it, or something. But what was really memorable were the feelings. There had been the anticipation. There had been the worry that I would crack up or run screaming or that some bastard of a Chinese would kill me. Then there had been the tension of the scene—the bullets overhead and men dying and the gun in my hand chattering like a woman on a telephone. And afterward, the gunfire dying down and stopping, there had been the calmness and a chance to relax. And there had been the sudden sure knowledge that I had been good, that I had held up, that I hadn't gone to pieces and wouldn't go to pieces. And that I was alive and had lived through the battle and would live through the war.

The same feelings were back again as I headed back toward the Malmsly. The night air was clean and cold in my lungs and I walked easily, confidently. I had set the first test up all by myself. I had staged a little incident for Crowley and I had brought it off properly. I felt sorry for the Canadian—he'd played a bit part in a private play without knowing what was coming off—but I wasn't going to waste tears on him. He was a means to an end and nothing more.

Maybe I had accomplished something. Maybe someone had noticed me and would want to know who I was. Because the person who chopped down the Canadian and kicked him in the head and left a dollar to clean his suit wasn't a slob with a chip on his shoulder. He was a heavyweight, a hotster, a definite mob type. He was Nat Crowley.

So maybe somebody noticed and would want to know more. If so, fine—that made everything that much easier. If not, also fine. Because the bit in the bar had still served a purpose. The incident had given me a crisis situation and let me play Crowley against it. I had learned new mannerisms and new manners. New pictures and new words.

I slowed down, stopped in a haberdashery doorway and got a fresh cigarette going. While I was lighting it, I managed to look around behind me. I learned something that way.

I had a tail.

He was around twenty-five years old. I had seen him before in the bar. Now he was following me.

It would have been easy enough to shake him but shaking him was the last thing I wanted to do. He was sizing me up, shadowing me to find out where I was staying and who I was. He would find these things out and tell somebody. Fine.

I shook out the match and dropped it to the pavement. I led my tail to the Malmsly. I got my key from the desk and took the elevator upstairs to my room. I washed up and went to bed, wondering how much the tail would have to bribe the desk clerk to find out who I was.

4

Wednesday and Thursday were waiting days, walking days, wandering days. Wednesday morning I took a rambling walk along the downtown east side. I watched the winos drink muscatel in broken-down bars. I passed through the fringe district, the borderland between Skid Row and Buffalo's version of Harlem. I looked at fag joints and porno bookshops and dubious nightclubs, all of them sad and slightly soiled in the daylight.

I stopped at a pawnshop and bought a gold signet ring that fitted nicely on the fourth finger of my right hand. I stopped at a cigar store and bet five dollars on a horse.

When I got back to the hotel the morning was mostly gone. The maid was making up my room.

"I'll come back later," she said.

"Go ahead and finish," I told her. "I'll stay out of your way."

I closed the door. She had already made the bed and was busying herself with a dustcloth, straightening up the dresser. I stretched out on the bed and watched her. She was a Negro girl, maybe twenty-five, maybe thirty. The contrast of her starched white uniform and her soft brown skin was dramatic. There's something about girls in uniforms that has always turned me on, Barshter or Crowley. Airline stewardesses, nurses—they always get to me. Maybe it's the lure of the forbidden or the idea that they're around to be of service.

So I watched the lines of her body, the taut muscles in her calves when she bent over to pick up something from the floor, the way her breasts pushed out against the front of the neat uniform.

The rush of desire surprised me. It was more than the lazy wouldn't-it-be-nice-to-get-into-that feeling that any man gets when he looks at a pretty girl. My feeling was hunger, raw and intense.

Don Barshter had never believed in the sanctity of the marriage vows. But Don Barshter had somehow never got around to cheating. He never started affairs because he was afraid they would be messy. And he didn't go to prostitutes because he was afraid of making his pitch to the wrong girl. If a girl had come along with the word *whore* tattooed in blue upon her forehead, square old Barshter would have taken her up on it. But he could go to a bar and sit next to a painted lady and never have the nerve to approach her.

But I wasn't Don Barshter anymore.

So I said, "You're a real pretty girl, honey. You know that?"

She looked at me. It was a look that would have scared hell out of Barshter but Crowley knew how to handle it.

"There's a fifty-dollar bill in my wallet," I said lazily. "Wouldn't take you more than ten or fifteen minutes to earn it."

Her eyes narrowed as she thought it over. She said, "Fifty?"

"Yeah."

"Anybody finds out, my butt is in a sling."

"Lock the door and close the drapes."

She locked the door and closed the drapes. She turned to me, her eyes uncertain, and said her name was Brenda. I grinned at her.

"Now let's see what's under that uniform, Brenda."

There was a lot of pretty brown skin under that uniform. She undressed quickly and I lay there watching her, enjoying the show. She wasn't wearing a bra, which I had suspected from the happy way she had bounced as she moved around. She didn't need a bra. Her breasts were young and upstanding examples of the form, coral at their tips. They were just a shade lighter than the rest of her, as if she'd lain out in the sun on her day off with the top of a bikini swimsuit covering them.

She stepped out of her panties and came over to me. She sat down on the edge of the bed and helped me out of my clothes. I smelled the hot female redolence of her. The girl stretched out on the bed beside me and our naked flesh touched. I let my hands enjoy the contours of her body. She lay obediently still, submissive, while I touched her breasts, cupped them, felt their weight. I ran my hands over her sweetly rounded buttocks and then traced them up the insides of her thighs where, for all that she was doing this for money, there already was the evidence of passion. My fingers found that tender spot and played their cunning game.

She purred like a lusty cat.

And then, because I was not Donald Barshter trying to coax love from his wife, because I was Nat Crowley being professionally serviced by an accommodating sweetness just out of uniform, I showed her how she would earn her money—to begin with. I put my hand on the top of her pretty head and eased her gently downward until she lay with her fine brown chest over my legs.

Then her eyes sought mine.

"Pretend you're a French girl, honey."

She knew the game as though she'd played it since kindergarten. Her lips were angel's wings, her tongue a ribbon of fire, her mouth a bowl of hot honey. She made it last a long time. And then I took over—Brenda had primed me. If she had primed me a moment more I wouldn't have been able to take anything over. As it was, I had to exert great control even though I was now taking Brenda in the most conventional of ways.

I wanted to end it up conventionally. The French stuff was

fine for a long preliminary, but for the payoff I wanted to be strictly in control, strictly in the saddle.

It was some saddle. It bucked and slipped all over the place and drove me nearly crazy. Which is the same as saying that Brenda wouldn't rest. Her hips were constantly in motion. Molten motion—and I think we were both practically delirious by that point.

We groaned together—and then we both lost control.

It was a moon shot with the softest of landings, and the last of it was an earth shot with an even softer landing because by then we had both had it.

When she was dressed and ready to go I grinned at her and gave her the fifty-dollar bill and an extra twenty. "For being so good," I told her.

Brenda paused at the door. "I make this room up the same time every day," she said.

"I'll remember that."

She started to open the door, hesitated and turned to face me. "I don't usually do this," she said.

"I know."

I showered, dressed and went down for lunch. I thought about the girl, how good she had been, how easily I had had her. And I thought about her last remark, that she didn't usually play for money. I believed her. Because not many men would have propositioned her that way. They would have thought of it, they would have wanted her, they would have formed the words of the proposition in their minds, but the words would never have been spoken and the girl would never have been possessed.

Donald Barshter would have ached for her. He'd have had her a thousand times in his mind and not once in the flesh.

It was a hell of a lot more fun being Nat Crowley.

After lunch I killed a few afternoon hours in a barbershop a few doors from City Hall. Donald Barshter used to save money on barbers—a haircut every three weeks, two bits for a tip and that was that. Nat Crowley ordered the works. The barber improved on my own shave, cut my hair, baked my face with hot towels. The manicurist held my hands and buffed my pretty nails. The shoeshine lad shined my shoes. It was a kick.

Then, Wednesday night, I found the bar.

It had taken a little looking but was worth the search because sooner or later I was going to make connections and the odds were good that this was going to happen in a bar. The right bar, the bar where Nat Crowley's kind of people hung out.

Well, this bar was called Cassino's. Red neon told me this. A slab of cardboard in the window supplied additional information—a jazz trio made noise weekends starting at nine-thirty, there was no minimum or cover charge, and Canadians were welcome.

And there we were. It was a quiet hole in the wall, an unobtrusive ginmill two blocks off the main drag. If you weren't looking closely, Cassino's was the same as bars on either side—nothing special, nothing remotely sinister.

I was looking closely. I saw four people inside. The bartender, a fat man who polished glasses as though they were the queen's jewels. A big flat-faced type who could only be a cop. Two thin dark knifeblades in flat black suits who could have played adjoining roles in Hollywood's latest exposé of the Mafia.

I went inside and took a stool at the bar. I ordered rye and soda and nursed it when it arrived. At nine-thirty a few more quiet little men filtered through the door from the street and took stools at the bar. At a quarter to ten the flat-faced cop stood up abruptly and left. At ten the bartender turned on the television and we watched the fights. Two welterweights were fighting at Saint Nick's in New York. I watched two dull rounds, then turned my attention back to my drink.

"You ought to watch this round," the voice said.

I looked up at the man talking to me. He was maybe forty-five, with soft, tired gray eyes, and he was twenty or thirty pounds overweight.

"There's no action," I said.

"This round," he told me. "The third. Porter gets to him in the third and the Mex goes to bed."

I lit a cigarette.

"The Mex dives," he explained. "And all I could get down is two C's on Porter. Watch. It ought to be cute."

It was very cute. We both glued our eyes to the set and watched Porter and the Mexican slide neatly into their act. I watched the Mexican miss a right cross and catch a left jab with his face. He stepped back sharply, looked shaky—and Porter went in for the kill. An overhand right put the Mexican down once for an automatic eight count. He got up, managed to wander into a left and two more rights and then go down and out gracefully.

The crowd loved it.

I said, "Pretty."

My friend turned and nodded thoughtfully at me. "So now my two bills is three-fifty," he said. "I had to give four-to-three. Porter's going places. They're moving him along slow, setting him up to keep the pot boiling. He ought to be ready for a title shot in eighteen, twenty months."

I didn't say anything.

"I think I missed your name," he said.

"Nat Crowley."

"Tony Quince," he said. We didn't bother shaking hands. "You new in town, Nat? I never saw you around."

"I'm new."

"New York?"

"I've been there," I said.

He digested this. "How about Chi? You been there?"

I nodded.

"And Vegas? And Miami?"

"All those places," I said.

"Who do you know in Buffalo?" Tony asked.

"Not a soul," I said. "I'm a stranger."

The bartender brought me a fresh drink. Tony Quince was drinking sour red wine. He emptied his glass and the bartender poured him another. Tony took a small sip, put the glass down and ran his tongue over his full lips. I found a new cigarette and put a match to it.

"You working, Nat?"

"Vacation," I said.

"Just passing through?"

"Maybe," I said. "Maybe I'll stick around. It's a nice town."

He worked on his drink and I worked on mine. The television set was off now and the room was quiet. A couple of high school kids wandered in and the bartender told them he wouldn't serve them. They left.

I finished my drink, picked up part of my change and stood up. I put out my cigarette.

"Later," I said to Quince.

He looked at me. "Sure," he said. "I figure we'll run across each other now and then."

I walked back to the Malmsly. There was no tail this time.

Thursday morning's paper told me that I was out five bucks. My horse had run third in a field of eight. I had my usual brunch in the Men's Grill and stepped outside. There was a pool hall on the second floor of an old building on Main next to a bus terminal. I walked up a flight of creaking wooden stairs, picked out a table and found a cue. A Puerto Rican kid racked the balls for me and I tossed him a quarter. He caught it in one hand, flipped it to the other and found a pocket to keep the coin in. I chalked my cue and broke the balls.

The place wasn't crowded. A few sharks tried to hustle each other. Two antique Italians who looked like retired barbers played three-cushion billiards. They were pretty good.

I wasn't. I stuck to aimless pocket pool and was lousy. I poked the balls around the table for half an hour. Nobody tried to hustle me for a game. A few kids, including the one who juggled quarters, looked me over out of the corners of their eyes. They were admiring my shoes.

When the game got boring I paid for my time and left. There was mail for me at the Malmsly desk. Two of my idiot letters had made the return trip, one from Chicago and one from Philly. The bank had sent over my checkbook, twenty-five pretty green checks, the name Nathaniel Crowley neatly imprinted in the lower right-hand corner of each. I stuck the checkbook in my pocket.

That night I went to a movie. I don't remember what it was about or who was in it. I sat in the balcony and thought about Nat Crowley and the way his little world was developing. I didn't waste much time thinking about Donald Barshter. There wasn't very much to think about. In four days he had managed to fade away to a shadow. Sometimes it was hard to remember what he was like, how his mind worked, how he spent his time.

It occurred to me that Barshter couldn't have been much of a guy. Too thin, too empty. In four short days he was all gray, all fuzzy at the edges. He must have been pretty useless to begin with.

I wondered if they had found Ellen yet. If they had buried her. And then I let those thoughts trail off. There were better things to worry about.

After the movie I stopped at a short-order restaurant for ham and eggs. Then I dropped in at Cassino's for a bottle of German beer. Nothing much happened there. I recognized a few men from the night before but nobody bothered to talk to me. Tony Quince wasn't there.

On Friday the wool farm came through with my new clothes. I put on a new shirt and a new tie and new shoes. I put on the gray sharkskin and left the lamp black and my original suit hanging in the closet. I got rid of my own shirts—they still had a Barshter laundry mark and there was no way I could keep wearing them. I scorched out the laundry marks with the end of a cigarette and stuffed the shirts into a paper bag. I carried the bag outside and found a trash can to dump it in.

The last concrete physical link with Donald Barshter was gone now, stuffed into a trash can and forgotten. I walked over to my bank and cashed one of my nice new checks. My wallet had been gradually emptying itself and I had to fill it up again. On the way out a little vice-president stopped me with half a smile and asked how Buffalo's weather compared with Miami's. I told him it was warmer down there but I couldn't complain.

I spent the afternoon going through motions that were becoming almost too familiar. I found a horse in the paper and bet another five on him. I walked around some more, catching an occasional nod from people I'd seen at Cassino's, people who had seen me. The picture was encouraging but hardly exciting.

There was a newsstand near my hotel that sold out-of-town papers. I resisted the temptation to ask for Barshter's home town paper and settled for a New York sheet instead. I went through it twice but couldn't find anything about Barshter and murder. I threw the paper away and ate a meal.

It was getting boring. I was slipping into a role neatly enough, putting on a new personality the way I had put on my new pearl-gray suit. But nothing was happening. I wasn't making the connections yet, wasn't hooking up with the people I was looking for. They nodded at me now and one of them had talked to me and somebody had taken the time to follow me once. But that was about all.

And something had to pop soon. For one thing, I had to find a way to earn a living. Nat Crowley spent his money freely and had to have it to spend. More important, I had to have a somewhat more permanent cover than the hard-stranger-in-town gambit. The gambit was effective but you couldn't make a lifetime out of it.

Anyhow, I treated myself to a thick rare steak in a wood-and-leather steakhouse and then headed for Cassino's. What the hell—at least that bar had music on weekends. I could drink my rye and soda with music behind it. And maybe something would happen.

Something happened.

But not at the bar.

As I was passing a basement coffeehouse that sent forth twelve-bar blues from somebody's guitar, a car pulled to a stop alongside me. An unmarked car, black, a year or two old. The driver pulled up the emergency brake but left the motor running. The man with him opened the door on his side and got out of the car. I waited for him, my hands at my sides.

He walked over to me. He was my age, my height. His hat had a longer brim than mine. His shoes were heavier and older.

I watched him put one hand into a pocket and come up with

a wallet. He flipped the wallet open and let me look at the flashing silver of a badge. He was a cop.

"Come on," he said roughly. "Get in the car."

I hunched into the car and sat next to the driver. The other cop came and sat next to me. I was the meat in the sandwich. The driver put the car in gear. We took off.

Nobody said anything. I wondered where I had gone wrong, how they had figured me out. And whether or not they still had the death penalty for murder in Connecticut.

5

Police headquarters was a dark red-brick building four stories high. Imitation gas lamps flanked the double doors at the top of a brief flight of heavy stone steps.

We parked across the street in a Police Only parking zone. The driver yanked the emergency brake again. This time he killed the engine. The other cop opened his door and motioned me outside after him.

"Come on," he said. "Move, Crowley."

I tried to keep relief from showing on my face. I tried not to react when he called me Crowley instead of Barshter. It was not easy. Maybe I managed it—it was hard to tell because the cop's face showed nothing.

I got out of the car. "Just for curiosity," I said, "what's the charge?"

"You're curious?"

"Yeah."

"Well, try mopery," the cop said. "Mopery with intent to gawk. How's that for a starter?"

"It's better than nothing."

He didn't smile. "Also suspicion. That's the official charge."

"Suspicion of what?"

We walked into the street to join the other cop, the one who had been doing the driving. "You ask a lot of questions," the first cop said.

"I just wondered," I said.

"Suspicion of conspiracy," he said. "Suspicion of conspiracy to commit a felony. It's handy, isn't it?"

I didn't say anything. We crossed the street. I was still a sandwich with a slice of cop on either side.

"What it all means," the first cop went on, "is we pick you up when we damn well please. That's the way it works in this city. You spend much time here and you learn that. You have to live with it, Crowley."

I didn't answer him. We climbed the heavy stone steps. I looked at the electric bulbs in the imitation gas lamps. The glass of the lamps was flyspecked. It needed washing.

We walked inside over a bare wooden floor past a desk. They didn't offer to book me. I didn't insist. We climbed another flight of stairs and found an empty room on the second floor. There was one chair in the room, a straight-backed wooden one. It looked uncomfortable.

"Sit," one of them said. I sat. The chair was uncomfortable.

For a good five minutes nobody said anything. The two cops lit cigarettes and smoked. I took out a pack of cigarettes, shook one loose, put it in my mouth. I scratched a match. The cops gave me time to take one drag. Then one of them lazily reached over and plucked the cigarette out of my mouth. He dropped it on the bare wooden floor and covered it with his foot.

"Why are you here, Crowley?"

"You told me to come. So I'm here."

"You're cute. Why Buffalo? What are you doing here?"

"It's a town. I always wanted to look at Niagara Falls."

"Who sent you, Crowley?"

"I came on my own."

"From where?"

"Miami."

They looked at each other, then at me. "We wired Miami," one of them said. "Miami police. They never heard of you down there."

"I live clean."

"I'm sure you do. Who sent you, Crowley?"

"Nobody sent me."

"What are you here for?"

"Laughs."

The one who had been the driver reached over to slap my face. My head caromed off the wooden back of the chair. I didn't say anything.

"Let's take it from the top," the first cop said. "You're a tough boy, aren't you? Hard as a rock."

"I'm easy to get along with."

"Uh-huh, You pounded a Canuck in a bar. A hard boy."

"Is he pressing charges?"

"No."

"Then why don't we forget about him?" They gave each other long-suffering looks again. They told me to stand up. I stood up. They patted me down to see if I had a gun. I didn't. They told me to sit down again and I sat.

"You're not heeled. You don't have a gun in your room. Where are you getting the gun, Crowley?"

"I'm making it with an erector set."

I got slapped again, harder. "Where's the gun?"

"There is no gun."

"Who sent you? Who are you supposed to kill?"

"I'm supposed to kill the President," I said. "I'm a Russian spy. I'm after bomb secrets."

That rated another slap. It was a hard one. I blinked a few times while the world came back into focus.

"I don't like you, Crowley."

I looked at him and waited for him to tell me why he didn't like me.

"I don't like hoods. I especially don't like imported hoods. We got plenty of domestic ones. We got homegrown hoods, tons of them. I don't like them, either, but at least they belong to us. They live here. They play all the local rules. I tolerate them."

"You're a tolerant guy."

"Yeah. I'm not tolerant of out-of-town talent. I don't like new people moving in, changing things around. It bothers me."

"Take a pill."

I got hit again but it was only a love-tap this time around. "All right," he said. "Let's start at the top again. Let's see what we can find out. We got all night, Crowley."

The cops didn't take all night. They took two hours and they went back and forth over the same ground until it was more a ritual than anything else. After a while they didn't bother slapping me anymore, which was just as well. I was starting to get a little punchy. I sat there and listened to questions I didn't answer. They milked the hard-guy routine until they managed to figure out I wasn't impressed. Then they kept going but their hearts weren't in it. Finally a young cop in a uniform came in and whispered something to one of them. The young cop left and my two grand inquisitors held an executive conference. They mumbled at each other, shrugged heroically and told me to get up.

We stepped into another room. I was photographed and fingerprinted. I blinked away the flashbulb image and wiped the fingerprint ink on the desk blotter. Then we left that room and walked out into the hallway and down the stairs to the main floor.

The cop who had been doing the driving the first time around found some fresh business and disappeared. The other grand inquisitor moved in for some fatherly advice. "Okay," he said. "Get lost."

"You're supposed to tell me not to leave town."

"I'll do the opposite. Leave town, Crowley."

"It's such a nice town. And the cops are exceptional."

He almost grinned. "I'm just an ordinary harness bull, Crowley."

"Sure," I said. "In an ordinary china shop. Take it easy."

I walked down the big stone steps to the street. The police force wasn't being too considerate. They drove me to headquarters but they were making me walk back on my own. I wondered how Barshter's home town police would feel if they knew that the Buffalo cops had just released Donald Barshter. That rated a grin but the grin was painful—my face was a little sore from the slaps.

I tried to decide what was supposed to be next on the agenda. The cops had found me and the cops had grilled me and the cops had let me go. When they had picked me up I had been on my way to Cassino's, on my way to see what would happen, to listen to three men make music and to wait for an opener. The cops had managed to toss the timetable out of kilter but Cassino's was still open and the music was still going round and round. I headed in that direction.

Friday night made a difference. The usual quota of stool-warmers warmed barstools and the bartender polished the same glasses all over again. But there was a piano and a bass and a set of drums on the little stage with three Negroes putting them to good use. The tables near the stage weren't empty now. About half of them were occupied, some with tweedy college types and their dates, others with older couples.

I handed the bartender a hello look and he nodded shortly at me. A handful of stool-sitters looked my way. Some of them recognized me and gave me a short nod. Others didn't and turned back to their drinks. I passed up the bar and found a table not far from the stage. I sat down alone, found a cigarette, lit it. They hadn't let me smoke at the police station and I hadn't got around to lighting one up on the way over. The smoke tasted good. I took a deep drag and held it in my lungs for a few seconds, then blew a cloud at the ceiling.

The music really wasn't bad. The drummer's timing was fine and the bassist set up a nice run of changes in the background. The piano player stayed away from long solos and worked on some fairly complex chord progressions. The song underneath it all was "Body and Soul," but you had to listen carefully to figure this out. I listened carefully and it was worth the effort. I liked what I heard.

Maybe I got lost in the music. My foot started tapping, picking up the rhythm all by itself. The cigarette sat between my thumb and index finger and burned itself up. And I didn't even notice the girl until she was sitting across the tiny table from me.

When I looked up at her she smiled. It was a nice smile on a nice face, neatly heart-shaped, with strong sound features. Her hair was black and her eyes were blue, a combination as perfect as it is rare. She was wearing very dark red lipstick and a little too much eye makeup. She was short and slender and probably twenty-five, give or take a few years.

"Hello," I said. "Have a seat."

"I already did."

"So you did," I said. "What else would you like?"

"Gin and tonic."

"That's a warm-weather drink."

"I'm a warm-weather girl."

There was probably an answer for that one but I didn't want to bother hunting for it. I turned around and there was the waiter, patiently waiting. "She'll have gin and tonic," I told him. "I'll have rye and soda."

He went away. My pack of cigarettes was on the table. She

took it, selected a cigarette, tapped it twice on the top of the table and put it to her lips. I gave her a light.

I said, "I didn't know they used B-girls here."

"I'm not a B-girl."

"Or hustlers, then."

She didn't frown. She smiled. "Or a hustler."

"Then what are you?"

"Just a sweet all-American girl," she said. "My name is Anne. Anne Bishop."

"Nat Crowley."

She nodded as if she had known this all along. "New in town, Nat?"

"Uh-huh."

"From where?"

"All over. Mostly Miami."

The waiter came back about then and put drinks in front of us. I reached for my wallet and he told me he would run a tab. I nodded to let him know that was fine with me. He left us alone again. The trio had moved into an up-tempo thing. The piano ripped off a harsh, driving solo, then stopped to swap four-bar choruses with the drummer. It was nice.

"You working, Nat?" Anne asked.

"No."

"Retired?"

"For the time being," I said.

"What do you do for a living, Nat?"

"This and that."

"And where do you do it—here and there?"

I nodded and watched her smile. Blue eyes and black hair and very dark red lipstick. Sweet small beauty against a background of smoky jazz. I sipped my drink and looked at her.

"This and that, here and there," she said. "You've got your

hand out and your fingers curled, Nat. You're looking for the connection." She paused and her eyes softened. "'The ancient heavenly connection to the starry dynamo in the machinery of night.' But I guess you don't read poetry, Nat. Do you?"

The phrase she quoted was from a long poem by one of the better clowns on the West Coast. I told her I didn't read poetry. And wondered how come she did and what she was doing at Cassino's and why.

"I didn't think so. Not a reader of poetry. But a very poetic person, in your way. Here and there. This and that. You have poetry in your soul, Nat Crowley. And I'm going to make that connection for you. You stay right here, Nat. You sit in your chair and drink your drink and listen to the music until a man comes to talk to you. And in the meantime I will make myself disappear."

She started to get up. I said, "How do I find you again?"

"Why should you want to?"

"To buy you another warm-weather drink. You hardly touched that one."

A smile. "Noomie's," she said. "An after-hours club. I generally hang out there from three on. The liquor's expensive but the music moves me."

"Better than these guys?"

She looked at the stage. The trio was working on "These Foolish Things," turning it into a slow gutty blues. "Much better," she said.

"Maybe I'll fall by. Any problem getting in?"

She was standing now. She looked at me, at my hat, at my shoes, at what was in between them. "Not for you," she said. "Not for you."

And then she turned on her heel and headed across the room. I watched her encase herself in a phone booth, drop a dime and dial a number. She talked for maybe fifteen seconds, then returned the receiver to the hook and left the booth. She walked out of Cassino's without looking back at me.

I traded my empty glass for a new drink and nursed it along in time to the music. I thought about Anne Bishop and her exit line with the little ritual that preceded it, the up-and-down look with the eyes bright and sharp. I wondered what she saw when she looked at me.

The trio tried "How High the Moon." A grubby little kid with a shoeshine box came into the place and pestered a few of the customers until the bartender told him to get the hell out. The kid got the hell out.

Questions.

Who was Anne? How did the outfit connections go together with the poetry and why was there so much makeup under the blue eyes? Where did she fit in and where was I going to fit in and where in the world did we go from here?

Questions.

I must have got lost—in the questions if not in the music. When the bit came I almost missed it. But not quite.

Two of them came through the door. They wore dark suits and dark ties and dark hats. One of them had a mustache. I saw the other one flash a look at the bartender. He gave a very gentle nod in my direction which I managed to catch out of the corner of one eye.

It was hard not to turn around. I let my fingers play with a cigarette and a match. I got the cigarette going and sat very still while they came over and took seats on either side of me. For a few minutes we let it lie. Nobody said anything.

"Crowley?"

It was the one with the mustache. I nodded a little and let my eyes look at him. His face showed nothing.

"We're supposed to take you with us. Mr. Baron wants to see you."

Their faces didn't show me a thing. I had never seen such a total lack of expression anywhere. At least the Mona Lisa is puzzling. Their faces were simply empty. They could have been taking me to meet Mr. Baron or to swim in the Niagara River. There was no way to tell.

And it was their party. I nodded again, put enough money to cover the tab on the table and stood up. The twins stood up with me. Mustache led me to the door while his buddy walked behind me. They took me down the street to a black Ford parked next to a No Parking sign. Mustache got behind the wheel. I sat next to him. The other twin sat next to me.

I wondered how long you had to live in this city before they let you sit by the window.

6

It took me three blocks to get lost. The street signs were invisible in the darkness but they wouldn't have meant much to me if I had seen them. I did figure we were heading west, but my knowledge of Buffalo's geography didn't take in the lower west side, which is where we went.

There was a river in that direction but we stopped before we got to it. We turned down a very old and very narrow street and pulled up in front of a sprawling brick house with a sad old elm in front. Mustache cut the motor. His twin got out of the car and motioned me to follow. I followed.

One of them poked the doorbell and we waited for something to happen. I glanced at the house and at the houses on either side of it. Baron's house was better than his neighborhood. The other houses needed painting and their lawns could have used a haircut.

A servant noiselessly opened the door. He looked at us and stepped back. Small eyes looked at us, eyes set close together in a broad forehead.

"We got Crowley," Mustache said. "Mr. Baron around?"

The servant pointed down a hallway. We stepped past him and he closed the big door behind us. We walked down the hallway, Mustache in front, me in the middle, and the other hood behind. The meat-in-a-sandwich gambit was giving me a complex.

The house was even better inside than out. The neighborhood was an old one and the house had aged along with it but, on the inside, carpets ran wall-to-wall and good mahogany furniture filled space nicely. There was a living room at the end of the hallway and we walked into it. The man in the big armchair looked at us without interest. He put his cigar in a big brass ashtray and waited.

"Mr. Baron," Mustache said, "this is Crowley."

The statement was unnecessary. I was very obviously Crowley, just as the mountainous man with black hair and heavy eyebrows could only be Baron. I looked at him and felt uneasy. He looked back, his eyes hard and sharp. He seemed incredibly powerful in a more than physical sense.

He didn't stand and we didn't sit. Baron picked up his cigar again and put it in his mouth. He chewed it and puffed on it and put it back in the big ashtray. When he spoke he didn't exactly talk. He rumbled.

"Your name is Nathaniel Crowley," he said. "You hit town Monday night. You're staying at the Malmsly. You got some letters, bought some clothes, went to some movies. You hang at Cassino's and act like you belong. A Canuck gets in your hair and you push his face in. The cops work you back and forth and you don't give an inch."

He stopped. Maybe I was supposed to be impressed. I wasn't. He knew all the things I wanted him to know, nothing more, nothing that he had had to sweat to find out.

"You don't pack a gun," he went on. "Not on you, not in your room. You give Miami for an address. Miami doesn't know you're alive. Neither does New York, neither does Vegas, neither does Chi. Or Los Angeles or Frisco. Nobody knows you."

He was a hell of a lot harder than my pair of cops. I didn't have a cute answer for him. Nothing but respectful silence.

"We made you at first for a gun. A trigger. But it doesn't add that way. You make too much noise; you set up too loud a front. You wander around and get yourself known. We thought somebody sent you to do a job on somebody but if they did you're the dumbest trigger ever. It doesn't add."

I didn't say anything. I was still standing and he was still sitting down. I wondered when he was going to offer me a seat.

"A floating hotster looking to put down roots. Heavy stuff looking for a home. Who in hell are you, Crowley?"

"You just told me."

"What did I leave out?"

"My mother's maiden name," I said, "and the amount of lint in my navel."

He looked bored. "Johnny," he said softly, "take him."

Johnny was Mustache's twin and he took me. I had less than a second to tense my stomach muscles before he planted his right hand in my gut. It wasn't enough time. I sagged in the middle and folded up just in time to catch his left with my face.

I had no time to think, just to react. I hit the floor and bounced back up with my face hanging out. Johnny tried to hang a right on it.

And missed. It was my turn now and I didn't miss. I put everything into a punch that landed a good four inches below his navel, which is as good a spot as any. He wasn't expecting it. He held on to himself with both hands and left his face wide open, I belted him and he hit the floor.

He started to get up and I had a foot back. I was just about ready to kick his teeth all the way down his throat when Baron's big voice stopped me.

"Stop it, Crowley."

I stopped long enough to look at him. He had a gun in his hand but he wasn't even pointing it at me. His smile was huge.

"Sit down," he said. "Relax, I got a job for you, one you should like. Steady work, easy work, and the pay is two bills a week. Sit down and we'll talk about it."

✿

"This bar," Baron said. "On the west side. Name is Round Seven. Ever hear of it?"

I shook my head. I was sitting in a chair near his, drinking rye and soda and smoking a cigarette. Johnny and Mustache sat together on a couch across the room.

"No reason you should of," Baron went on. "Just a bar—no music, no floor show, no hustlers. It was a fight mob bar. That's where the name comes from. Now there's just three or four fights a year so there's no fight mob. The bar has a neighborhood trade. A guy comes in for a quick beer, that kind of bit. Right now it's closed."

I took a final drag on my cigarette. I blew out smoke and then leaned over to stub out the cigarette in an ashtray. I relaxed in my seat and sipped my drink.

"Round Seven," Baron said. "It changed hands. For five years the place slips downhill, loses a little dough every year. So some people in Cleveland buy it. A corporation. It's got this big tax loss behind it and the corporation stands to make a profit on the bar even if it loses money. You understand?"

I nodded.

"So it's a tax loss," he said. "It's other things. Sometimes it's handy to own a nice quiet place where nothing much happens. A quiet neighborhood bar with a quiet neighborhood trade. Very small, very quiet. You understand why something along those lines might be handy?"

"A front."

The big head moved in a nod. "A front. Or a drop. Or whatever you want to call it. Say two or three guys need a place where they can talk, a place nobody nosy knows about. Or say somebody has a warm package and wants a cool place to park it for a while. Or say anything. This bar is two things. A tax loss and a handy place. But you understand all that."

I watched him take another cigar from the cedarwood humidor on the table next to him. It was wrapped in a cellophane wrapper and he unwrapped it carefully and methodically. He crumpled the cellophane and dropped it into the copper wastebasket beside his chair. I thought he was going to bite off the end of the cigar and spit it into the wastebasket. He didn't. He took a tiny gold knife from his jacket pocket and cut the end of the cigar. He put the knife away and lit the cigar with a wooden match.

"You ever tend bar, Crowley?"

"No."

"Nothing to it. The Polacks who go to Seven don't ask for anything fancy. A shot, a beer. Most you have to do is toss the shot into the beer for the lazy ones. No tricky cocktails, no food to serve, nothing to mess with. You're open six nights a week, Monday through Saturday, open at seven and close at three. The pay is two bills a week, a little over ten grand a year. Think you can handle it, Crowley?"

I look at him. "You're handing me the job?"

"If you want it."

"Why?"

His smile was a lazy one now. "Let's see," he said. "Say there's this hotster from nowhere who hits town with his eyes open. A heavy type but none of the heavyweights know him. Too big to ignore. Big enough so he has to be on the right side or not around at all." I finished my drink.

"This hotster," he said. "He can't just hang in the middle of the air. The town is nice and neat, no trouble and no heartache. The right people take care of each other and the road is smooth and soft. What you got to do is take this hotster and find out what he wants. Then you hand it to him and you're friends. So you're this hotster, Crowley. I'm guessing all you want is the inside track and two bills a week for a soft touch. I'm guessing you know the game and you play the right rules. Did I guess right?"

I wondered what would happen if I said no. I didn't want to find out.

"You guessed right."

"I usually do. So you'll be a part of us and we'll have a piece of you. If you save your money we can throw nice things at you. You got five grand you can spare right now?"

I didn't.

"Too bad," Baron said. "There's this con mob out of Denver that needs fast money. They've got a rag ready to go and they ran out of capital. They're small time but the payoff is pretty. Five grand now buys twenty when the con goes through. If it goes through. The risk is there but the odds are nice."

He took the cigar from his mouth and studied the tip of it. He looked at me again. "Round Seven is closed now," he said. "I think it opens up on Monday. That all right with you?"

"Sure."

"Fine. You meet Johnny at Cassino's around dinnertime Monday. He'll have the keys and run you over there. Sooner or later you'll want a car, right?"

I nodded.

"You'll get a good price when you're ready to buy. We take care of our own." He smiled again. "This time you get a chauffeur. Johnny runs you over there Monday. He'll fill you in on the details. There's nothing to do but open and close, take the money and make the drinks. Deliveries are all arranged for. It's no worry of yours."

I nodded again.

"All you have to do is nothing, Crowley. A check comes once a week in the mail. The check is from Ruby Enterprises. That's the corporation that owns Round Seven. The check is a hundred a week. You steal the other hundred from the till."

I must have looked puzzled. "Two reasons," he said. "One, it saves you money. The yard a week you steal is tax-free. Two, it looks better in the books. If Ruby pays a guy two bills a week to tend bar in a losing business somebody might wonder. This way it's just another hundred lost."

"I get it."

"I thought you would, Crowley. That's all there is. You do your job and no more. If there's something special for you to do you'll hear about it. Don't ever call me and don't ever come here unless I ask for you. Monday, dinnertime, Cassino's, you meet Johnny. Goodbye, Crowley."

Johnny and Mustache dropped me off at my hotel. This time the heavy stuff was over. I sat up front with Mustache while Johnny spread himself all over the back seat. They even talked to me.

Mustache's name turned out to be Leon Spiro. Johnny turned out to be Johnny Carr. I told Johnny I was sorry I hit him and he told me he was sorry he hit me. We were practically necking by the time they let me out of the car. I watched them drive away. I stood on the corner and smoked a cigarette. A cab came by and I hailed it. He stopped for me and I got into the back seat.

I told him to take me to Noomie's.

"That's a pretty rough neighborhood, Bud. Sure you want to go there?"

I told him to just drive. I made my voice hard and flat and there must have been something in it that made him crane his neck around to look at me. I don't know what he saw in my face but it was enough.

He turned around and drove in chilly silence through dark streets. He didn't talk any more.

7

I paid the cabby and tipped him. He drove away and left me alone with the night. The streets were empty. There were no signs of life anywhere but I could feel the presence of people—doorway sounds, back-alley sounds. Soft sounds and an undercurrent of tension below the placid surface.

Noomie's didn't look like much. A white frame house, a red-and-green sign that winked in neon with the name of the place—and nothing more. A few years of dirt kept the windows opaque.

I crossed the street and knocked on the door. After a few seconds it opened. The girl at the door was a shade lighter than the maid at the hotel. Her figure was good, her eyes very tired. Behind her in shadows I could make out a dark Negro built like a boulder. The girl looked me over and wound up with her tired eyes on my face.

"I don't know you."

"Crowley," I said.

"It rings no bells," she said.

I looked beyond her into a too-dark hallway. "Anne Bishop here?"

"Big blond girl?"

"A little brunette. And you can stop playing games, sweetheart."

She grinned softly and pointed past the bouncer, toward the darkness. I walked that way and nobody stopped me. The darkness lasted a long time and then gave way to a large low-ceilinged room that wasn't much brighter. A handful of red and green unshaded bulbs on the ceiling gave the room an odd Christmas-tree look. I lit a cigarette, shook out a match and dropped it to the floor.

People sat at tables and drank. There was a four-man combo on a very small stand—piano and bass and drums and tenor saxophone. The tenor was in the middle of a long, liquid, moody solo. They had a small spotlight beamed at the stand and it showed how smoky the room was.

I picked up a rye and soda at the bar and then looked around for Anne. I almost missed her because for some reason I thought she'd be sitting alone, waiting for me. She wasn't. I found her at a small table over on the left with Tony Quince.

I walked over to them. There was a third chair at the table and I took it. They both said hello to me.

"Nat Crowley," Quince said. "Long time."

"Just a few days."

"You making out all right?"

"I can't complain."

Quince was drinking sour red wine again. I saw him sip his drink, set it down and let his face relax into a slow, easy smile. "Where you been?"

"Here, there. I thought I'd run into you at Cassino's."

"I only go when I want to watch a fight," Quince said. "Porter goes again a week from Wednesday. He's up against somebody name of Jackson. You could do worse than go along on him."

I thanked him for the tip. We talked a little more, listened to more music. He finished his wine and put a few singles on the table. He stood up.

"Got to run," he said. "Later, Anne. I'll see you, Nat."

I watched him leave and wondered who he was. Then Anne leaned across the table and took another of my cigarettes. I gave her a light and she blew a little smoke in my face.

"Like the music?" Anne asked.

"Uh-huh." I looked at the taut lips, the blue eyes. "I didn't know you knew Tony."

"I know everybody," she said.

"You belong to him?"

It was hard to tell whether she was angry or amused. "I don't belong to anybody, Nat. I'm the chick who walks by herself. Straight out of Kipling, with a twist."

"All right," I said.

"I did him a favor tonight. I ran him an errand. I like to do favors for people."

"You did me a favor," I said. "Thanks."

"It worked?"

"It worked."

"I just ran a little interference," Anne said. "I just made a connection. 'An ancient and heavenly connection.'"

The poem again. "So now we're 'dragging ourselves through the Negro streets at dawn,'" I said, "'looking for an angry fix.'"

She was very surprised, very confused. Something was out of place in her calm little scheme of things. "You know the poem," she said. I nodded.

"That's weird," she said. "You're no beatnik. I don't get it. You just read Ginsberg for kicks?"

"A hobby. Everybody needs a hobby."

"Sure. Who are you, Nat? Where do you fit in?"

I shrugged. "Just a hotster looking for a place to be cool."

"Sure. A man from here and there looking to do this and that. You're complicating things, Nat. You're breaking the pattern. People aren't supposed to do that. They're supposed to stick to stereotypes. It's easier that way."

"You're building castles," I said.

"You think so?" Her eyes said the liquor was reaching her. It didn't make her giddy or sloppy. Just sadder, deeper. "You don't understand, Nat. Everybody has an image. They hand it to you or you pick it out for yourself in a department store. Then you hold on to your image and live with it. You can't get tricky with an image. It's what you are."

"And you? What's your image, Annie?"

"Annie," she said. "Nobody calls me Annie. Maybe I like it. I'll have to let you know."

They brought us more drinks. She was still cooking with gin and tonic. I stuck to my rye and soda.

"My image," she said. "That's easy, Nat Crowley. My image is the little girl who grew up too fast. Little girl burning her candle at both ends because it sheds a wondrous light. Little girl getting dizzy in fast circles. And not giving a damn."

"How little?" I asked.

A blank look.

"How old, Annie?"

"Twenty-two," she said.

"You look older."

"I'm supposed to. Part of the pattern. I'm supposed to look older because I've grown up so fast and am so world-weary. That sort of thing."

"Part of the image?" I asked.

"Part of the image."

"Uh-huh. And what's underneath it?"

There was a moment of softness. Then tension tied up the mouth and the eyes hardened slightly.

"Oh, the hell with it," she said. "Let's dance, Nat."

We danced, we drank, we danced. It was easy to lose track of the time and everything else. They didn't believe in letting you nurse a drink at Noomie's. They brought you a fresh one as fast as they dared, and they dared once every five or ten minutes. I would have got very drunk if they had put a full ounce in each drink. They didn't come close.

But I couldn't resent it. An after-hours spot is a tough operation. You have to grease the local law and the state liquor authority boys at the same time. It's expensive.

So it was a few minutes after five, maybe later. We were back on the postage-stamp dance floor and we were dancing, if you could call it that. The song was slow and bluesy. Anne was in my arms, dancing close, her head snug against my chest, the perfume of her hair reaching my nostrils. It was good perfume.

"Nat…"

I looked at her.

"Don't tell me too much, Nat. It's all a contest, all a test of leverage. All a question of the upper hand. Don't tell me too much."

"Too much gin and tonic?"

Her eyes cleared. "Maybe," she said. "Maybe. Hold me close, Nat."

I held her close again. Something made me think of Ellen. Nothing specific, nothing concrete. Vague and patternless thoughts that I pushed from my mind.

The music ended. We found our way back to the table and drank the two fresh drinks that were waiting for us there. I crooked a finger at the waitress and she gave me the tab. It was an impressive one. I put a lot of money into her hand and she didn't even think about bringing me change.

"Come on," I said to Anne. "I'll run you home."

"I didn't know you had a car."

"I don't. I'm good at getting cabs."

We left the nightclub and walked out into sunshine. People were getting up to go to work. The neighborhood looked much worse, now that I could see it. Paintless frame houses yawned at the sun and looked ready to collapse. Garbage cluttered the street and the yards. The shirts and underwear on everybody's clotheslines were ready for the rag barrel.

"God," Anne said. "It's bad enough in the dark. We should have left earlier. Let's get out of here, Nat."

I caught us a cab and she gave the driver her address. The cab took off and we slid into silence.

Her lipstick had worn off and her makeup was smudged, maybe from dancing with her cheek against my jacket. She looked a little like a whore in church except that there was a strange cloak of innocence that covered her and kept her pure. Maybe Anne was a saint in a whorehouse. So, even though I wanted to touch her, to take her hand, to kiss her, I did none of these things. I waited.

In a little while the cab pulled up in front of a dingy brick building five stories tall. We turned and looked at each other. I wanted to say something clever but nothing occurred to me. Her mouth opened, and she hesitated for several seconds. "All right," she said finally.

I waited.

"All right," she said again. "Pay him, Nat. Pay him and come upstairs."

I paid him and tipped him. We stepped out of the cab onto the sidewalk. We didn't hold hands or exchange soulful looks. I followed her up the stairs and through the doorway and waited while she opened the inner door with her key. Her apartment was a fourth-floor walk-up and we climbed all those stairs in silence.

Her apartment wasn't much but it looked livable. Anne had an Oriental rug on the floor and Miró prints in plain black frames on the walls. The living room held a coffee table, a couch, two chairs and a table with a hi-fi on it. There was no television set. There wasn't room for one.

I waited while she put the latch on the door. When she turned around a part of her mask fell away and I could see more of her. She was frightened.

Not of me, not of what was coming next. It was more a fear of something within herself than a fear of a tangible experience. But she looked so horribly afraid that I had to reach for her—and that did it. She came to me soft and soundless and burrowed her face in my chest.

I spoke her name.

"Hurry," she whispered. "No words. The bedroom's right through there in the back. Please hurry."

I picked her up and carried her there. She was easy to carry. I put her down on the edge of the bed and stood looking at her.

"The light," she said, pointing.

I couldn't remember turning it on. But a cord dangled from a bare bulb on the ceiling. I yanked it and the room was darker. There had been no preliminaries. We held each other briefly, then parted. We undressed ourselves in darkness and silence.

When we were naked together I reached for her and the physical contact of our bodies was electric in intensity.

We met in pure blind need. I felt her body beneath me, her small breasts cushioning my chest, her arms locked hard around me, her legs fastened around my hips.

In the silence and darkness our bodies battled together. I felt her nails in my back, her teeth in my shoulder. The union was neither slow nor gentle. It began quickly and rushed forward like a young river plunging for the sea.

It was more animal than human—blind and hungry and desperate. We were caught up in fury and need and love and hate and fear. There was nothing held back. There was nothing but our mutual race to the top.

Once during the race we changed positions. Just once. I think she wanted to feel something like a sacrifice. So, her dark hair hanging over her eyes, she did it so that it looked as if she were impaling herself.

The sensation was something like being sucked in and then expelled. What it was like for Anne I'll never know, except that she did have that expression on her face of being a sacrifical offering on an altar.

Of being in an agony.

Her face twisted in a grimace each time she sank down on me to the hilt. I worried her swollen nipples each time she went through that act.

Several times she flung her head back, her thigh muscles corded in the extremity of her body's arching, and a kind of high whine came from her throat.

It was almost too much for me. So I flipped her back to where she had been at the start, with Nat Crowley dictating matters.

Then there was no longer that sacrificial expression on Anne's face. There was only a look of fierce oblivion, eyes shut tight— and Anne shouting obscenities as I made the plunges through center.

We reached the heights together. For a slice of time everything dissolved and the world went away. Then I rolled free of her and we lay on our backs in the darkness and listened to our ragged breathing.

"I get up at noon," she said a little later. Her voice was flat, spent, empty. "Be gone before I wake up, Nat."

I stayed at her side until I was sure she was sleeping. Then I dressed in the darkness and went back to the Malmsly.

8

Thursday night at the Round Seven. The fourth night of an easy, lazy job. The middle of the second week in Buffalo.

It was raining outside and the rain made the crowd lighter than usual. Only four of fifteen stools were filled and all three of the wooden tables were empty. A man in faded Levi's and a loose flannel shirt sat tossing off shots of bar rye and chasing them with short beers. A pair of skinny kids, soldiers home on leave, sat drinking draft beer and boasting about women. An old drunk worked his way slowly but surely through a bottle of Corby's.

There was no television set and no juke. The last owner had left a small radio behind the bar. I turned it to the one station in town that hadn't been taken over by adolescents and soft music played. I polished glasses.

The man in faded Levi's chased his final shot with his final short beer, stood up and left. The soldiers stopped lying about women and went out looking for some. The old drunk ordered another shot. I pushed his money back at him and made it on the house. He smiled and swallowed rye.

A sweatless, painless job. So far Round Seven was nothing but a tax loss for Ruby Enterprises. No packages had come, no messages had been given or received. There was a small steel safe in the bar's back room but for the time being it stayed empty. I wondered what would be put in it later on.

The drunk asked for another rye. I poured it and let him pay for this one. I tossed the dough in the cashbox without ringing it up. That was where the second half of my two hundred a week came from, money that never went through the bar's books in the first place.

Soft. The right people said hello to me at the right times. The cops let me alone whether they liked me or not—I was local, I fitted, I belonged. My name was Nathaniel Crowley— that was the way I signed my checks and that was the name on the Bartenders' Union card in my wallet. A friend of Baron's had arranged the card.

A newscast came on the radio and I switched to another station. I caught the tail end of a commercial, a station break, some friendly words from a friendly disc jockey. I poured another shot for the drunk and wondered when he would fall off his stool. The disc jockey stopped talking and played a record. The door opened and Tony Quince came in.

He walked to the far end of the bar and parked himself on a stool. I took my time getting to him. I stopped on the way to pour out a glass of the sour red wine he liked. I gave it to him and he smiled at me.

"Working hard?" he asked.

"Not too hard."

"Nobody should work too hard. Life is too short. You play poker?"

"Sometimes."

"There are a few fellows having a game tonight. Soft action, just stud and draw for table stakes. Small table stakes most of the time. You drop fifty and you're the big loser. I thought maybe you'd like to play."

"Who's in?"

"Berman and Bippy and Moscato and Weiss. You know them?"

I knew Berman from an evening at Cassino's. I didn't know the others.

"I quit at three," I said.

"We start at three-thirty. Fair enough?"

I told him it was fine.

"You got a car yet?"

"I get one the middle of next week," I said. "It's on order." It was a Lincoln convertible that someone had stolen from a doctor in Santa Monica. It was costing me about half the book price and they were shipping it into town Tuesday or Wednesday unless they hit a snag.

"I'll pick you up then. Three o'clock?"

"I can grab a hack."

He shook his head. "No trouble for me," Quince said. "It's on my way, stopping here. And we can talk on the way. You and me, we have things to talk about. Maybe."

I told him three was fine. He took his time with the sour wine and I let him alone from there on. A fellow came in with a girl who looked like somebody else's wife. I gave them rye and ginger ale and they took the drinks to a table. The next time I looked their way the guy had his hand up the girl's skirt.

The girl was squirming around in her seat, her eyes glazed over with passion. Her mouth dropped open and she looked as though she wanted somebody to put something in it. The guy kissed her mouth and kept his hand busy. She locked her plump thighs around his hand and rocked back and forth, moaning softly. I wished they would get the hell out and go to a motel. Round Seven wasn't licensed for a floor show.

Tony Quince finished his wine and left without saying goodbye. The old drunk left too. He said goodbye and walked out on wobbly legs. A few more people drifted in and out. The guy with somebody else's wife stopped playing little games and took her home to one bed or another. It got to be three o'clock and I closed up for the night.

Quince drove up just a few minutes after I finished locking

the front door of the bar. He leaned across to open the car's door and I got in next to him. His car was a Cadillac, an old one, made before they ruined everything with tail fins. I closed the door and he drove.

"Berman lives in the suburbs," he said. "But first we talk."

"We can go to my place."

"You still at the Malmsly?"

I shook my head. "The Stennett."

The Stennett was a fine old residential hotel. I had three rooms and a bath. The hotel service was fine and the rent was not too steep.

The Stennett had everything I needed, including my little chambermaid from the Malmsly. She had switched jobs when she had found out I was moving—the pay was as good at the Stennett, the work no harder, and she knew I was good for a fifty-dollar bill each time we fell into bed. I was seeing Annie now and then but I didn't see what difference that made. I still had a thing for women in uniform, and breasty Brenda filled out the black-and-white Stennett uniform nicely. And when she got out of it she knew just what I wanted her to do and just how to do it...

Quince said, "Let's stick to the car. I don't have too much to say."

That was fine with me.

"I'm not going anywhere special," Quince said. "The car goes by itself. Just driving, so we can talk."

"Sure."

"You met Lou," he said after a pause. "The guy who handed you the job at Round Seven. I mean Lou Baron."

"I met him."

He nodded, as much to himself as to me. "I set that up," he said. "You meeting him, I mean. I told Anne she should hang around Cassino's until you showed and then call Lou and set up a party. I told Lou what I knew about you and that he ought to tie you in with what's happening. I arranged things, you might say."

"Thanks."

He shook his head impatiently. "Don't thank me—just listen. You know anything about me? Or about Baron?"

"Not much. I guess he runs things. I don't know what you do."

He turned the Caddy onto a side street heading back toward Main. It was easy to see that he and the car knew each other. His hands moved lazily and the car did everything he wanted it to do.

"Yeah," he said, "Lou runs things. You could put it that way."

"And you?"

"This and that."

I didn't say anything. I took out my cigarettes and offered the pack to him. He shook his head and I lit one for myself.

"I got a few things going," he said. "A horse room downtown, a few phones, a few people to answer them."

We crossed Main again but in a little while he swung a sharp right on a street that ended at a cemetery. Then he drove the Caddy into the cemetery.

"I come here all the time," he said. "Late at night, early in the morning. It's peaceful. You can talk. If it bothers you…"

"It doesn't bother me."

"To some people it's spooky. But I was talking about the things I have going for me. Part of a few roadhouses out on the lakeshore. And some legit stuff. Moving vans, vending machines. Stuff like that."

I looked out the window at an imitation Washington's Monument with a cross on the top. Something ran across the Caddy's path and disappeared into shrubbery. It looked like a rabbit but it was hard to tell.

"You know what's happening in this town, Nat?"

I shrugged. "A little. Not much."

"All calm on the surface and all set to boil underneath. The cops handed you a hard time, Nat. A pair of bulls named Zeigler and Kardaman. They put you through the wringer. You know why? They thought you were an imported gun. Talent from someplace coming into town to do a job. A job on Baron."

"They thought I was hired to hit him?"

"To hit him in the head. To give him an extra mouth."

There was very little to say to that.

"I'll take a cigarette now, Nat."

I gave him one. He lit it with the dashboard lighter and blew out the smoke without inhaling. We were still driving around and I was getting an unguided tour of the cemetery. He was right—it was peaceful as hell.

"Lou's a funny guy," he said. "He's been big for ages. A hell of a long time to ride tall. He made friends, he made enemies. That's what this is all about, a matter of friends and enemies. Your friends stay big and you've got everything nailed. Your friends fall on their faces and you fall on top of them."

I threw my cigarette out a window. It missed a tombstone by a few feet and landed in wet grass.

"Baron had friends," Quince went on. "One of them got shot in a barbershop. You remember that one?"

"I remember."

"Other friends. None of them got picked up at Apalachin. The boys there didn't invite Baron's friends. You understand?"

I nodded.

"So Lou is in a little trouble," Quince continued. "Right now things are cool, everybody smiles at everybody. The governor's been throwing this state crime commission at everybody, he wants to be president or something, and nobody sticks his face out. Everything is cool. This won't last forever. They're cool now, they'll be warmer later."

"And Baron?"

"Dies," he said.

He let the word sit there and float in the air. It was the right word in the right place. I looked out the Caddy's window at a million graves, each one neatly marked, each one as cold as death. I saw a hole where someone had been digging a fresh one. I thought suddenly of Ellen. Then I thought about Baron again—who was going to die.

"Not today, not tomorrow, maybe not this year. But soon. It's a matter of friends, a matter of who has what kind of leverage. This whole business is a business of levers, of who has what hold on who. But all the bricks are going to fall on Baron. No choice. Even he knows it."

For a few minutes I didn't ask the question. "What's your angle?" I finally said.

"Baron dies. Somebody has to be the new Baron."

"You?"

He shrugged. "There are other guys. There's also me. We wait and see."

"And why tell me all this? What's my angle?"

He shrugged again. "It's all a matter of friends," Quince said. "I said that before. I got some friends. I can use other friends. I don't know much about you. All right, I don't have to know much, I'm not asking you your religion. What I know, I like. I like your style."

"Thanks."

"When Baron falls, I might need you."

"So?"

The palms spread upward. "That's all."

"My father told me never sign a contract. Not even a verbal one."

"So you had a smart father. But there's no contract, Nat. I didn't bring a contract along. Not even verbal. Just things to say, just information so you can start thinking about things. That's all."

"Uh-huh."

"We can be friends," he said.

"We're friends now."

"Better friends. We can do each other favors. And if things break right after Baron goes, you could sit in a nice spot. You could do worse."

"I probably could."

We drove out of the cemetery. He must have known the place pretty well. We were on Main now, heading north. I had got lost the minute we entered the cemetery.

"So we talked," he said. "So I told you things and you listened. That's all. Now let's find Berman's house and play poker. I feel lucky tonight."

We played cards around an octagonal table in Mel Berman's recreation room. It was a small and pine-paneled room in the basement of his ranch house in a middle-class suburb of Buffalo. We played stud and draw. Nobody had much to say.

Berman ran an appliance store in one of the city's shopping districts. The appliance store lost a little money every year. Berman made money because he wrote numbers and booked horses when he wasn't busy selling television sets and dishwashers. His family didn't know this.

The Bermans belonged to a synagogue and country club. Berman's wife worked on fund-raising committees. His daughter went to dancing class at the synagogue. His son was a sophomore at a public high school. Berman loved his wife and his son and his daughter.

The game was going when Tony and I got there. It didn't break up until eight or nine in the morning. Somewhere around seven-thirty Berman's wife came in with a tray of food. She gave us scrambled eggs, toast, jelly, coffee. The food was good. Berman apologized for the lack of bacon, told us his wife kept a kosher kitchen.

A little while before we called it quits Berman's son came in to say goodbye to his father. His name was Sanford, Sandy for short. He and his father were buddies.

"Take it easy on the broads," Berman told him. "You can catch more than a cold."

Sandy punched Berman on the arm. "Watch out for him," he told all of us. "He draws to inside straights."

We went on playing. I wound up around fifteen bucks ahead for the evening. Then Tony drove me back to the Stennett. We didn't talk on the way, at least not about Baron and how he was going to die. We coasted on small talk and he let me off at the hotel. I walked inside, went upstairs and climbed into bed.

When I woke up a few hours later a warm hand was rubbing my back, massaging the nape of my neck. I rolled onto my side and opened my eyes.

Brenda was smiling down at me.

"You said I was to come around this morning," she said.

I mumbled something.

"You want me to come back in a few hours?" But tired as I was, I wanted her anyway. I told her to get undressed and I rolled over on my back and watched as she took off her clothes. Her body looked better every time I saw it.

"You know what to do," I said, closing my eyes. "My wallet's on the dresser. Help yourself to fifty before you go. And take it nice and slow now, and put me back to sleep again."

I lay there, more asleep than awake, and she did all the things she was supposed to do.

I fell back asleep again. I never even heard her leave the room.

9

It was my second Sunday, my second day off. I crawled out of bed somewhere in the middle of the afternoon and found my way to the phone, which was ringing. It was Anne Bishop.

"That date of ours," she said. "It's still on?"

I shook my head to clear it, which hurt. The night before I'd been Round Seven's best customer and an even better customer of an after-hours joint called Moon High. Now my head was the size of a basketball and ached.

"Date," I said.

"You were going to take me for a long ride. And dinner."

I remembered. "An hour," I said. "I'll pick you up."

I put the phone to bed and turned into the bathroom for a shower and a shave. I cooked water for coffee and drank it scaldingly black until things settled down between my ears. I put on a new suit and a sincere tie, and went downstairs.

I slipped into a restaurant around the corner for breakfast. I sat at a table and ordered bacon and eggs and some more coffee. The coffee was grim—I tried to drink it without tasting it. I looked at my watch. It was time to get Annie.

The watch was pancake flat, the size of a half dollar. Lou Baron had given it to me a couple days ago. First there had been a phone call one afternoon telling me about someone who owed money and hadn't paid. I had gone to the address Baron gave me, had found the guy and had beaten him up. I had used fists on his face and feet on his ribs. The next day somebody had dropped off a package at Round Seven and had told me it was for me. The watch had been inside. Engraved neatly on the back was the legend, *To Nat from Lou Baron,* in tiny script. The watch even kept time.

The sky outside was seven various shades of gray. I went back to the Stennett and told the doorman to find my car for me. He brought it out from the garage and I gave him a dollar. I looked at the Lincoln and smiled. It was low and lovely with plenty of spirit under the hood. I got behind the wheel, put the top down and looked up at the gray sky again. I turned a key in the ignition and drove to the house where Annie lived.

I hit the horn. Time passed while she hurried down four flights of stairs. Then the front door flew open and she ran down the walk to the car. I opened the door for her and she bounced into the seat beside me.

She was wearing brown loafers, black tights, a soft brown skirt and a black cashmere sweater. She looked like a wood nymph. "A ride in the country," she said. "It sounds like a groove."

"It's the wrong day for it."

"That doesn't matter, Nat. I want to look at trees and smell fresh air. I want to get high on oxygen. And it's not a bad day."

I told her it would probably rain.

"I hope not," she said. "I like this car with the top down. Wind blowing my hair around. I like it."

We drove around looking for the country and we couldn't find it. We took one of the principal streets straight out of town and that didn't do any good. It was just a big city street that kept on in the same vein even when the city stopped. We tried other roads, still looking for the country, and we found everything else. We found housing developments and school districts and country clubs. We found highways and freeways and throughways and causeways. We did not find the country.

"Oh, hell," she said. "We're halfway to Albany, I think. This isn't working out, Nat."

"Should I turn around?"

"I guess you might as well."

I found a Texaco station and pulled in for a transfusion. He wiped my windshield, checked my oil and water, filled my tires. I gave him a credit card and he performed rituals with it. Then I turned the Lincoln around and aimed it at the city again.

"There used to be country," Annie said. "The city ended at the Kenmore line and after that there was country. I used to live just inside the city line. There were big vacant lots to play in. Now they're all ranch houses."

She stretched out a hand. I lit a cigarette and put it between her fingers. She took a very long drag and blew out smoke.

"We used to go for drives in the country every Sunday," she went on, "when the weather was nice. Pack a picnic lunch, spread a tablecloth or a blanket and eat outdoors. Or my old man would build a campfire and we would bake potatoes in the coals and grill steaks over it. None of the charcoal briquette stuff. Just a plain wood fire. My brother and I went around picking up dead wood and my old man would build a fire. Now they have anti-fire laws and everybody has a brick barbecue in the backyard and there isn't any country anymore. Just a chain of suburbs running from Buffalo to New York. Let's find some place that cooks rare steaks and makes big drinks. I want to get high, Nat."

So we found a place just outside of Buffalo whose decor was colonial American, with hardwood Windsor chairs and ladderback barstools and plenty of wooden timbers holding up the ceiling. Anne got going with a double gin and tonic and had two more before they brought the food around. We passed up steak and settled on roast beef, which seemed to be the special. They brought us each a big slice an inch thick with roasted potatoes and creamed spinach on the side. Afterward I had brandy and she had more of the gin and tonic. She shot high as a kite.

"There's no country anymore," she said. "Isn't that rotten?"

"You still playing that song?"

She had eyes like an owl. "It's not a song. It's the sad truth. Nothing is the way it used to be. It never is. I don't belong here, Nat."

"Where do you belong?"

More gin. "In a bus called Limbo on a one-way street. Going the wrong way. You remember those houses we passed today? The split-levels?"

I remembered ugly houses set row on row, like crosses in Flanders Field. They all looked different, with different paint jobs and different landscaping—but they also all looked the same.

"In a suburb," she said. "In a fifteen-thousand-dollar split-level trap with a husband in my pocket and a baby in my uterus. Picture this. The husband works for a big company. His salary isn't too great but they have a dandy pension plan. I have charge accounts and heavy furniture and a washing machine. And my bridge game is lousy but it's something to do while you trade platitudes."

It sounded familiar, I thought. It was Donald Barshter's life.

"Where I belong," she was saying. "By the book, by all the rules. The rules fell flat. You know why? Because I started liking jazz. All right, that's easy—you find the husband and you make him build a stereo rig in the basement recreation area. But I liked jazz the wrong way. I went to clubs. I met men and I talked to them. I'm a good listener. I learn things."

She was smoking a cigarette. It fell from her fingers and started to scorch the linen tablecloth. She didn't notice it. I picked it up and put it out.

"So I learned a subculture. Isn't that handy? I learned a subculture. I learned there were things happening that didn't happen in split-levels. I learned that some people get along without a pension plan. And I found out something. Annie Bishop just couldn't make it in a split-level. She couldn't swing with the bridge-and-canasta set. She'd be living in a world without colors."

She started to drink more gin and tonic. I took the glass away from her and told her to go easy. She pouted at me, then forgot about the drink.

"That split-level," she said. "That imaginary split-level. I took it and I put a sign on it. Know what the sign said?"

"What?"

"That's easy," she said. "It said, 'Annie doesn't live here anymore.' Like the song. Buy me another drink, Nat."

She had one more drink and went over the edge. She made the john just in time and came out a few minutes later with a green look. I paid the bill and steered her outside to the car. I drove her to her apartment, carried her upstairs and undressed her for bed. By then she was out cold. I wedged her under the covers, tucked her in and turned off the lights.

When I got outside again it had started to rain. I put the Lincoln's top up and drove back to the Stennett. I turned the car over to the doorman and went inside. There was a message for me at the desk, a number to call. I didn't recognize the number and called from the pay phone in the lobby instead of from the phone in my room. I didn't want to go through the switchboard.

I didn't recognize the voice that answered. I told it who I was. Then there was silence for a minute, and then there was Baron's voice. "Nat," he said. "Glad you called. Get over here, will you?"

I told him I would. I went back outside and got my car back. The doorman was puzzled but he decided to humor me. Then I drove over to Baron's house.

I parked in front, got out of the car and nodded at the sad old elm tree. I rang Baron's bell and the beady-eyed servant opened the door. He led me to the living room. Johnny was sitting on the couch and Baron was in his chair. I sat in the chair I'd used before and Baron offered me a cigar from the cedarwood box. I passed it up. He unwrapped one for himself and used his little gold knife on it. Then he lit it and smoked.

"Everything okay, Nat?"

"Everything's fine."

"I called five-thirty, maybe six. You were out."

"I was with a girl."

Baron laughed. "That's good enough. How's everything at Round Seven, Nat? Somebody drop a package there?"

"There's one in the safe now."

"That's good. A guy'll be by Thursday or Friday to pick it up. Meanwhile it sits. You know what's in the package?"

I shook my head.

"You want to know?" he asked.

"It's none of my business."

He laughed again. "You got a good attitude, Nat. Straight and simple. How's that watch work?"

I looked at my watch. "It works fine."

"Keep good time?"

I nodded. "I like it," I said. "Thanks."

"What the hell," he said. "You did a good job. Smooth and proper. I like your style, Nat."

He liked my style—and Tony Quince liked my style. I didn't even know I had one. I watched Baron set the cigar in the ashtray and open the gold knife again. He ignored me for the moment and concentrated on cleaning and trimming his fingernails. He still had that tremendous aura of power. It wasn't the sort of thing you got used to. It grew, the more you knew him.

He was going to die and Tony was going to take his place. I wasn't sure I believed that.

"Ever been to Philly, Nat?"

"I've been there."

"You know the town?"

"A little."

That satisfied him. He nodded thoughtfully and went on trimming his nails. Then he folded the knife and put it away again. He picked up the cigar. It had gone out and he scratched another match to relight it.

"There's this plane," Baron said. "Leaves two, two-thirty in the morning, gets into Philly around three-thirty, quarter to four. Johnny's holding a ticket for you. It's a round-trip ticket. The return is open—you make your own reservations. Depending on how much time you need."

He said that much and stopped. It was my turn to ask a question. I decided to wait him out.

"Guy meets you at the airport," Baron went on. "He knows what you look like, a general description. You wear a black bow tie and make things a little easier for him. He'll pick you up, finger the contract for you. How you do it is up to you."

"What am I supposed to do?"

He looked surprised or pretended to. It was hard to tell which. "There's this other guy," he said. "You hit him. Johnny's got a nice clean gun, can't be traced, you can pitch it down a sewer when you're done. You look funny—something the matter?"

"I don't want it, Lou."

"You want a drink? You nervous?"

"I don't want the job."

"Porky," he called. "Make Nat a drink, huh? He likes rye and soda, not too much soda." We sat there not saying anything and Porky mixed me a drink and brought it silently to me. His dark face was absolutely expressionless. I sipped the drink.

"Drink okay, Nat?" Baron asked.

"It's fine."

"Not too much soda?"

"Fine."

"You want the job," he went on, in the same tone of voice. "It's a pretty deal. Philadelphia called up, said there's a job to do and please send a man. I owe Philly a favor. And it's nice, it's pretty. Not an important hit, just a punk with large ideas, a wise punk who's getting in the way. The price is five grand. That's a very good price for such an easy hit."

"I still don't want it."

"You still don't want it. You hot in Philly or something?"

"No."

"You're too rich to have a use for five grand?"

"That's not it. I'm not a killer. And I don't want it."

His eyes narrowed and we looked at each other. He smoked his cigar and I drank my drink. There was tension in the air, static electricity hovering in the room. We went on looking at each other.

"You're not a killer, Nat?"

"No."

"You never killed anybody? I don't mean in a war, that doesn't count, it's not the same. I mean killing that's not legal."

I didn't say anything. I thought about Ellen and had trouble looking into his lazy eyes. They weren't so lazy anymore.

"I can see it," he said. "The way you move, the way you talk, the way you act. You killed people, Nat. You sure you didn't?"

No answer.

"I told you I'd throw good things at you," Baron said. "This is a good thing. You aren't going to turn it down and throw it back in my face, are you?"

I had taken the soft touch at Round Seven, the watch with its inscription, the car at a price. I had taken the good clothes and the good apartment and the good money. This was part of the package.

I said, "Who's the contract?"

"Nobody," he said. "A nobody named Fell, Dante Fell. A collector who started holding out. Who did this too often. Who never learned."

I stood up. "Where's the ticket and the gun?"

Now he was smiling. "Johnny," he said, "give Nat the ticket and the gun. The gun is an automatic, Nat. You familiar with an automatic?"

I nodded. Johnny gave me a gun and a round-trip airline ticket to Philadelphia. I put the ticket in my wallet and the gun in my pocket.

"The reservation's in the name of Albert Miller. You'll be back here in plenty of time for opening up at the saloon tomorrow night. There won't be any follow-up from Philly. If there is, you were with a dozen guys who were with you every minute of the time. So there's no trouble."

I nodded. I picked up my glass, finished the drink. I put it down on a table and Porky took it away to the kitchen.

"You aren't angry, Nat. Are you?"

"Why should I be angry?"

"About the job. You still don't want it?"

I managed to shrug. "It's a job," I said. "And the price is nice."

I could have gone back to the Stennett. I could have stopped at a bar and had another drink to take some of the high-wire tension out of my system. I could have picked up a convenient whore for the same purpose.

I did something else.

I drove to the nearest drugstore and shut myself up in the phone booth. Then I put in a call to Tony Quince.

10

He answered on the second ring. I heard his hello, then music and a girl giggling in the background. I said, "No names. Is your phone okay?"

"I don't think so," Tony Quince said. The girl giggled again and he told her to shut up. Then he said, "How about yours?"

"I'm in a booth."

"Give me the number," he said. "I'll call you back."

I gave him the number and he rang off. I lit a cigarette and sat in the booth waiting for something to happen. The phone rang again before I had finished the cigarette.

"Fine," he said. "Now we're both in phone booths. I hated to leave that broad there. She'll turn my place upside down. You sound nervous."

"I am."

"Let's have it."

I dropped my cigarette and stepped on it. "I just saw Baron," I said. "He's sending me to Philly on a two-thirty plane."

"What for?"

"For a hit."

He whistled. It sounded funny over the phone. "Who?" he asked.

"Somebody named Dante Fell. Baron said Philadelphia wanted him to send somebody and he owes them a favor. I get five grand for it."

"That's a fair price," he said. "What do you want to know?"

"I want to know what's happening."

"Makes sense. Dante Fell—it rings sort of a bell, come to think. Can you stay right where you are? In the booth, I mean."

I looked around. Nobody seemed interested in my phone booth. The drugstore was almost empty. "I don't know," I said. "The guy might close for the night. Either that or he'll try renting me the booth by the month."

"I'll make it fast, Nat."

He rang off again. I felt like some kind of a nut sitting and waiting for the phone to ring so I held the receiver to my ear and kept the hook down with the other hand. I mouthed a long imaginary conversation and waited.

He called back five, maybe ten minutes later. His voice was urgent.

"I got to talk to you, Nat. Not on the phone. In person."

"We're both in booths."

"This has to be in person. I know a bar on the other side of town, nobody ever went there who can count past three, there's no hassle. Meet me in a back booth as fast as you can. This is big."

He gave me the name and address. I left the booth and headed the Lincoln toward the place he had mentioned. I parked around the corner on a street no one ever drove on. I didn't want anyone recognizing the car.

Tony was waiting in the booth. The bar was almost empty and the few men and women around weren't speaking English. I joined him in the booth and he pushed a beer at me. He was drinking beer himself instead of sour red wine.

"I won't drink the wine they sell here," he explained. "And you don't want to try the rye they sell here. But it's safe and it's quiet. Baron is working funny angles, Nat. I'm glad you called me."

"What's up?"

"What do you think?"

I shrugged. "I'm a stranger in town," I said. "I don't know a thing."

"I called Philly, Nat."

"And?"

"They didn't order a hit." My mouth must have dropped open because he was grinning at me. "Not the boys I know in Philly. Not the boys who run the town. The hit was ordered, sure. By Baron's friends. The ones on the outside looking in."

I didn't say anything. It was starting to get cute and I wasn't sure I liked it. It was interesting, anyway. I sipped beer and waited to find out more.

"Dante Fell is a bookie. He doesn't get along with some of Baron's friends in Philly—he doesn't like them and they don't like him. If he's getting hit there's a reason. It's a power play, Nat. These Philadelphia people, these friends of Lou's, are starting to push. Lou is backing their play. He's giving them a man for a hit. This means they've got his support."

"What's his angle?"

"They're his friends. If his friends run Philly, this makes Baron a bigger man. It also makes him a more secure man. So he's backing them, sending you down to pull a trigger, betting his dough on them. He loses."

"Why?"

He drank beer, made a face. "I hate this stuff. If a man is going to drink he should drink wine."

"Why does Baron lose?" I wanted to know.

"Oh," he said. "Yeah. Baron loses because his side has kings instead of aces. He's got second-best hand, and that doesn't even get its ante back. A lot happens in Philly this week. A lot of Baron's friends are going to die. Not a war, not a blood-bath—there aren't that many of them. Four, five hard boys. They die."

"Was this set all along?"

He shook his head. "But it's set now. Because you called me. I told Philly and things move fast."

I didn't say anything. Maybe it had been stupid, calling Tony Quince. Or maybe it was smart.

"That's part of it," he went on. "That's the part that doesn't matter too much because what happens in Buffalo and what happens in Philadelphia are different things. I figure this is a good time for things to happen in Buffalo. I figure Baron dealt the hand, Baron gave the order sending you to Philly, Baron ought to be ready to play. You see what I mean?"

I saw what he meant.

"He's been big a long time, Nat. And now that throne is wobbling all over the place. It could get pushed."

"By you?"

"Yes."

We waited each other out. This time I talked first. "This is interesting," I said. "All of it. One question."

"Where do you fit in?"

"That's the question."

He sipped beer again and made a face again. "Well, hell, Nat," he said. "That's all up to you. You can join either side because right now you sit in the middle. You can play for either team. You can bet on the winners or the losers. It's all up to you."

"Keep talking."

"What you got to do is simple. You got to decide where you want to stand. You can decide you're better off with Baron. So you get up and tell me, well, it's been fun. Then you run like hell to Baron's place and tell him what happened. You say Tony Quince is a fink, he's no good, he's looking to push you out and make trouble. You tell him you happened to spill to me and I told the boys in Philly what happened. Then he pushes me out

of the picture, gets the word to his friends in Philly to lie low—
and you're his fair-haired boy. He likes you."

"And when he asks why I talked to you?"

"You were being smart. You were finding things out. You had
an idea I was ready to buck him and you wanted to check it
out."

I thought it over. "Okay," I said. "And suppose I pick the other
side. Then what happens?"

"You go to Philly, right on schedule. You pick up your fingerman in the airport and take a ride with him."

"And shoot Fell?"

He frowned. "Don't be silly. You couldn't do that even if you
wanted to. Fell knows what's happening now. No—you go on a
ride with your fingerman. Then you kill him. Just put a bullet in
him and leave him somewhere. Baron gave you a nice clean
gun and you use it."

"What happens when Baron hears about it?"

"He never hears a thing. He's not expecting you to make the
hit until sometime in the morning or afternoon. You make it
right away, get the first plane back. He's off balance. We move
very fast. We get together and the wheels start to roll. We've
got surprise on our side and Baron's up the nearest creek. You
follow me?"

"I follow you."

He finished his beer. Mine was still half full. I let it sit on the
table in front of me and turn flat. I took out my pack of cigarettes
and offered him one. He took one and I took one for myself.
We smoked.

"If you pick my team," he said, "and if we win, you could have
it made."

"Tell me about it."

"The local organization would go along. It's like South America.

The whole system stays the same. The only change is who's on top."

"A palace revolution."

"You got it. The organization stays in line. Baron goes, Scarpino goes, that pair of hoods he's got working for him goes. That Johnny and that Leon. You know them?"

He meant Johnny and Mustache. I told him we'd met.

"They go, one or two more go. Then things change and at the same time they stay the way they are. You get out of the Stennett and buy yourself a big house. You trade that Lincoln for a Caddy or a Rolls."

"I like the Lincoln."

"So keep the Lincoln. Don't play word games, Nat. You know what I'm talking about."

"I know."

"You side with me and we win, you're right up there on top next to me. That's a hell of a lot of bread and a hell of a lot of power. It's the town by the short hairs. You could do worse."

"Probably."

"Or you could bet on Baron. And wind up tending bar at a higher salary, getting a bonus here and there. Or he could lose and you could get killed."

"I take that chance either way."

"Sure," he said. "I could lose and you could get killed. Getting killed is something that could happen either way. It's a risk. You can't look at the risks in this business. They're always around. You got to look at the rewards. You want to tend bar forever?"

"It's a good job."

"But not a very big one. There are bigger."

I put out my cigarette. The smoke was scorching my lungs and my throat. "I could have gone straight to Philly," I said. "I could have shot Fell dead as a lox and flown back and the hell with it. No sides to take, no wars to start."

"You could have."

"But that's over now. Now I have to pick a side. Now there are two sides and I have to pick one of them."

"Yeah."

"Well," I said. I stood up and stepped away from the booth. "Take it easy, Tony. I'll see you."

11

The flight left Buffalo at two-eighteen A.M. The rain had eased up by then and what was left of it didn't bother the pilot at all. I had a seat over the right wing. I was wearing a black tie and I had a gun in my jacket pocket.

The stewardess offered me magazines but I wasn't interested. Instead I let her keep bringing me cups of good black coffee. Not that I was in any danger of falling asleep. But the coffee speeded things up, made the connections in my brain take shape a little faster, a little easier.

It wasn't real yet. It was a dream, say, or a high school play, or one of those gangster pictures I used to watch, or some other illusion that had nothing to do with reality. The plane was a movie set standing still, the gun in my pocket a prop loaded with blanks.

So I pushed the gun and the whole routine out of my mind and sat there concentrating on the stewardess. She was a green-eyed redhead with a figure that looked good despite the tailored blue uniform she wore. Her pretty pink skin looked just as good in that uniform as Brenda's did in hers. But there was a point at which I could no longer concentrate on the stewardess, so somewhere in the sky between Buffalo and Philadelphia I went to the john to get rid of some of the coffee. I checked the gun there, too. It was a big gun, a heavy gun, a Browning Parabellum with a thirteen-cartridge magazine. It must have weighed two pounds. I took the magazine out and practiced with the empty gun, sighting at imaginary targets and squeezing the trigger. I hadn't fooled around with this sort of weapon since basic training, a long time ago. I liked this gun, the weight of it, the feel of it. It was a shame I was going to have to leave it in Philly.

I put the magazine back, tucked the gun away in a pocket and went back to my seat. At three-thirty-seven the pilot put the plane down on the runway at Philadelphia International Airport. It was a lousy landing, bumpy and jarring. For a minute I thought the gun would go off in my pocket. It didn't.

It was cold in Philly but there was no rain. I got off the plane and headed across to the terminal. My fingerman was waiting for me. He looked me over, noted the black tie and decided I was his man. He came over to me.

"You Crowley?"

I nodded. Fingermen are supposed to be small and shriveled, with ferret faces and shifty eyes. He was six-four and he was fat. He was wearing a plaid lumber jacket and heavy cordovan shoes. He looked stupid.

"My name is Garstein," he said. "You're supposed to come with me."

"Sure," I said. "Wait here a minute."

He waited there while I found my airline desk and looked for a plane back to Buffalo. There was one that left at four-fifteen, a non-stop flight. That gave me a little less than three-quarters of an hour, which was fine. I made reservations on it. I used the name Albert Miller again, the same name I'd had coming in from Buffalo. A pretty blond took the reservation and thanked me. I told her it was a pleasure.

I went back where I had left Garstein and he was waiting dutifully. "You're supposed to come with me," he said again.

"I know."

"I show you this Dante Fell bum. He's a punk. A wise punk."

"You talk too much," I said.

He looked at me and turned his mouth off. I was the trigger and he was the finger so he was supposed to be respectful. He kept his mouth shut and led me from the terminal to a parking lot where his car was parked. It was a Plymouth with a crimped fender. He got behind the wheel and I sat next to him on the front seat. He started the engine, pulled the car out of the lot and drove off down a highway.

"How far to the city?"

"Not far. A mile, two miles. Used to be that the airport was way out in the country. The city spread."

The road we were on was a wide one, a busy one. There was traffic even at three-thirty in the morning. It wouldn't do.

'This Dante Fell—"

I told him to shut up again. He did for a minute but then asked if he should get some music on the radio. I told him I didn't like music. He gave a sad shrug and went on driving.

There was a crossroad up ahead. "The next right turn," I said.

"What about it?"

"Take it."

"It's out of our way," he said. "This is the best route."

I put my hand in my pocket and found the gun. I cocked it and put a bullet in the chamber under the hammer. "Take the turn," I said.

"Somebody following us?" He looked doubtfully in the rear mirror. Then he turned to look at me.

I took the gun out and let him see it. His eyes became very wide and his face pale. I said, "Garstein, you talk too much, you ask too many questions. Take the turn or I shoot you."

He wondered about it for a minute. The car slowed down and we turned at the intersection. It was a quiet road, not any traffic in either direction.

"Now what?" he asked.

"Drive," I said.

He drove about the length of three city blocks. Then I told him to pull the car off the road. He didn't want to but when I shoved the nose of the Browning into his fat neck he did what I told him to.

"I don't get it," he said. "I just don't get it."

"You don't have to."

"Baron sent you. Lou Baron, from Buffalo. Right?"

"Right."

"To do a job," he said desperately. "On Fell, Dante Fell. Not me. I'm nothing, I'm nobody, I'm Jack Garstein and I don't count for a thing. You got your signals crossed, Crowley."

"You still talk too much. It's a lousy habit."

"God damn!"

"Get out of the car, Garstein."

He did not want to get out of the car. He tried talking some more but I poked him with the gun. He got out on his side and I crawled across the seat and followed him onto the road. Then we walked around the car and stood in some farmer's field.

"You're gonna shoot me," he said. "You're gonna kill me."

That didn't deserve an answer.

"Crowley, there's a car coming. You can't shoot me— they'll see you. You can't."

"So we wait until they pass."

I watched him think. He was trying to get up the nerve to run out into the road and ask them for help. The car came. There were two kids in the front seat, high school kids looking for a place to park. They drove past us and Garstein didn't move.

I pointed the gun at him.

"Please," he said.

"Shut up."

"Crowley…"

It still wasn't real. I was a machine, primed and ready. It wasn't real.

"I'm a married man," he said. "I got a wife. A kid, a little girl—"

"You got insurance?"

He looked blank.

"Everybody should carry insurance," I said. "Plenty of it. It's a great comfort in times like this."

He didn't understand.

"You should have met me before," I said. "I would have sold you a policy. Straight life, twenty-five thousand dollars' worth. Then you wouldn't be worried now."

He still didn't understand. His mouth opened and closed. He took a step back and I squeezed the trigger. I shot him four times in the chest and once in the face. I wiped my prints off the gun and threw it in the bushes. Then I got into his Plymouth and drove back to the airport to catch my plane.

I was back in Buffalo by five-thirty. The sky was gray with dawn and the air was moist and warmish. I used a pay phone at the terminal to call Tony Quince.

"I'm home," I said.

"Get over here fast, Nat."

"Right away."

I found a cabby, gave him Tony's address and told him to hurry. I settled back in the cab and tried to relax. It didn't work. There would be a time to relax again but not for a while. I looked in my pack for a cigarette. The pack was empty. I bummed a cigarette from the cabby and smoked.

Tony lived in a third-floor apartment in a four-floor building. It was a good building, grounds well kept, inside clean and moderately plush, I rang the bell marked Quince and an answering buzzer let me open the vestibule door. I walked up the stairs and wound up in front of a door with a brass nameplate that had Tony's name on it. The door opened before I had time to hit the bell.

"Come on in," he said. "Sit down. How was Philly?"

"I didn't see much. Just the airport and a stretch of road."

"How did it go?"

"It went."

"Easy?"

"I suppose so."

I wasn't sitting down. Neither was he. I stood like a robot while he walked back and forth, in front of the window. I joined him at the window. He had a view of private homes across the street. An unexciting view. There was a bird singing his head off in an elm tree across the street. I wished he would shut up.

Quince said, "I guess you picked a team."

"I guess so."

"Mine."

"Yours."

"It's the right side, Nat. The winning side, the side that pays off. You used your head."

"I hope so," I said.

He came back from the window. "The finger," he said. "Where did you leave him? You dumped him, huh?"

I told him what I had done with Jack Garstein. This pleased Quince.

"They won't find him right off," he said. "They won't find him for hours—they won't expect Fell to get hit for hours. By that time so many things are going to happen in Philly that Baron won't know Jack Garstein from Abraham Lincoln."

"There's a similarity," I said. "They both got shot."

He got a laugh out of that one. He broke the laugh off abruptly and turned serious. "We got to move fast," he said. "I told you before a few people got to be hit. You remember?"

I remembered,

"Baron, Scarpino, Johnny and Leon. You know Scarpino? Forty or forty-five, thin, ugly. One eye doesn't work too good. You know him?"

"I don't think so."

"He's very close to Lou. He's got to go. Hang on."

He strode to the phone and picked it up. He didn't look fat and dumpy now. He was taking charge, moving in, and it showed in his voice and his bearing and his walk. I wondered why he had ever seemed soft and easygoing. He dialed a number and spoke quickly to someone named Angie, his voice low. He put the receiver down and looked at me.

"Angie Moscato," he said. "Remember?"

"From the poker game."

"Yeah. He can use a gun and he can drive like hell. He's on his way over here now. This is how we do it, Nat. First we pick off the flies. We cut the arms off and then we go for the head. Scarpino first. He lives with his old man. The old man sings anarchist songs and makes wine in the basement. He's old and senile. So we get Scarpino right there."

I let him talk. He was doing fine.

"Then Johnny Carr and Leon Spiro. Spiro keeps a broad maybe two blocks from Cassino's. He'll be there now, at the broad's. So will Johnny."

"They'll both be there?"

"Yeah. They share the broad." I made a face. "Share and share alike," Quince said. "They're a pair of pigs and the broad is a third pig. We ought to hit her just for exercise.

"And then Lou," he went on. "The big one for last. That's the tough one. He sleeps with one eye open and a gun next to him and he never eases up. But this is the time for it. We take the others first. Then we figure out a way."

I found a chair and sat in it. He went into his kitchen and came out with a full coffeepot. He poured out two mugs of ink and gave me one of them. I burned my tongue on it but I drank it anyway.

"I got bennies," he said. "If you need them."

"I don't use them."

"Neither do I. They let you move fast but they get you too keyed up, too high. Coffee's plenty."

We drank the coffee. He stood up again and walked over to a dresser, opened the bottom drawer. I watched him rummage around in a pile of shirts and sweaters. He came up with two revolvers, thirty-eights. He hefted them both and handed one to me. It was a Smith and Wesson, a little lighter than the Browning automatic I'd used before.

"It's full and it's safe. Good enough?" he asked.

"Fine."

He kept looking in the drawer, found a shoulder holster and got into it. He put the gun in place.

"I haven't got an extra rig," he said.

"I don't use them," I said. I put the gun in my pocket.

He poured a little more coffee. We drank it down. Then he stood by the window waiting for Moscato.

"There he is," he said finally. "Let's go, Nat."

12

The three of us sat in the front seat. We didn't do much talking. It was getting close to six-thirty, according to the watch on my wrist, the watch that had *To Nat from Lou Baron* across the back. I didn't feel much like looking at the watch just then.

The excitement was the main thing. You could see it in Angie Moscato's hands on the wheel, in Tony's eyes. Moscato drove swiftly and easily but his hands were curled around the steering wheel like snakes. We were all on a roller coaster, on a train, on a boat to hell. We couldn't get off. We could only ride to the end.

The sun was coming up now and it looked as though it were going to be a good day—bright, warm and clear.

Scarpino lived with his father in the heart of the very old west side near the waterfront. There was a housing project stretching for a block in one direction and another going up on the other side. But where Scarpino lived was an area still untouched. Dirty frame houses were clustered together. Grass and weeds grew between the blocks of cement and cracked them. Angie parked the car in front of a house that looked a little better than the others.

"Don't know why he lives here," he said. "He makes good dough. He could live better."

"It's his old man," Tony said. "He doesn't want to leave the old neighborhood."

"This is a good one to leave. He must be a nut." We got out of the car and left the motor running. Tony led the way up the driveway to the side door. Angie took a gun from his shoulder holster and kept it in his coat pocket. He didn't take his hand away from it. Tony rang the bell and we waited until a man opened the door.

He was short and scrawny. He had a drooping mustache and watery eyes. He wore dirty denim overalls and a starched white shirt open at the neck. His eyes danced. He knew Tony.

"Tonio," he said. "Buon giorno, Tonio." There was some more in Italian that I couldn't catch.

Tony said, "Buon giorno, Mr. Scarpino. Is your son at home?"

"He sleeps, Tonio. He sleeps all morning."

"We have to see him, Mr. Scarpino. You wait right here, Mr. Scarpino, while we go see your son."

We left the little old man in his kitchen and went up a squeaking flight of stairs. I said, "Won't the old guy remember us?"

"He doesn't talk to cops. He hates cops and priests. He learned that in the old country and never forgot it. Scarpino is here."

We went into a messy little bedroom. Scarpino was sleeping under a thin blanket. He woke up, blinked and started to open a drawer in the bedside table. Moscato closed it on his hand. Scarpino didn't yell. He lay down in bed again and put his bruised fingers to his mouth.

Tony said, "Get up and get dressed, Scarpino."

"Why?"

There were three guns pointed at him. He looked at each gun in turn. Then he focused on Tony.

"Why me, Tony? We get along. We been friends for—"

"Cut it. You and I hated each other since 'forty-eight. Get up and get dressed."

Scarpino got out of the bed and into his clothes. He took a tie off a hook in his closet and started to put it on. Tony took it away from him.

"Forget it," he said. "You don't need a tie."

"You want to be Number One, huh, Tony? Want to push Lou out?"

"You're smart today."

"You'll never make it. You know why? You ain't got the guts it takes. You're soft inside."

Tony turned the pistol around and held it by the barrel. He laid the gun butt along the side of Scarpino's cheek. He hit him with it on the other side of the face. A trickle of blood came from Scarpino's mouth. Scarpino wiped it away with his shirt sleeve.

The old man was waiting downstairs. Scarpino was made of wood now. He didn't talk, didn't make extra moves. He went to his father and began speaking slowly in Italian. I asked Tony what he was saying.

"Telling him he's going on a trip, Nat. He'll be gone a long while and the old man shouldn't worry."

We left the house and walked down the skinny driveway to the car. Angie got behind the wheel. Scarpino didn't want to get in—he stood next to the car without moving until Tony poked him in the ribs with the gun. Then Scarpino climbed in. Tony sat next to him and I got in back. Angie started the car.

"Where now, Tony?" Scarpino's voice had lost the toughness. He wasn't whining yet, but it was close.

"Angie knows where." Quince turned and grinned at me. "This is cute, Nat. You'll like this. And it's still early enough."

"Tony—"

Scarpino got the pistol butt over the jaw again. He didn't ask any more questions after that. Angie gunned the car and then headed north. It wasn't long before he whipped into the entrance of the cemetery where Tony Quince and I had had our little talk.

Tony was laughing now. "You get it, Nat? I told you I like this place—it's peaceful, quiet. I set this up earlier, sent a few boys over with shovels. It's cute, Nat."

Angie knew the way. He drove over a variety of little roads, pulled over and stopped. A fresh grave yawned at the sky, a raw brown mouth in the earth. Scarpino saw it and went dead white. It was all real for him now.

It was tough getting Scarpino out of the car. He didn't want to go. A pair of guys stood beside the grave and leaned on shovels. They smiled at Tony and he waved a hand at them. They watched as we dragged Scarpino over to the open grave.

Angie Moscato shot him. He wrapped his pistol in a car blanket to muffle the noise and then put the muzzle about six inches from Scarpino's face. He squeezed the trigger and there was a soft wet popping sound. Scarpino fell down dead and Tony kicked him over into the grave. We all walked to the edge to look at him. Most of his face was missing. My stomach was a huge hard knot.

The pair with the shovels looked at Tony. He looked back at them for a second and then gave them a nod. They put the shovels to work on the mound of earth alongside the grave. The first shovelful landed on Scarpino's chest. The three of us turned together and walked away from the grave. I could hear the rhythm of the shovels, and the sound of dirt covering Scarpino.

"Five years," Tony said. I looked at him, "Five years ago I bought the plot, the cemetery plot. I bought it under another name, paid cash for it. You do that and the plot's yours forever. Whether you use it or not, it's yours. A handy deal. Pay now, die later."

He laughed at his own joke. Moscato and I did not laugh. Tony stopped suddenly. He reached out one hand and I gave him a cigarette. I cupped my hands, scratched a match and gave him a light. He inhaled deeply.

"So I bought it five years ago," Tony said. "For Scarpino, for whenever the time came. Now he's in it. Now they cover him up and put the sod back on top. He's gone, all gone. Just one more fresh grave and the only way anybody knows something's wrong is checking the map. How many people sit around reading graveyard maps?"

I lit a cigarette of my own. It was getting brighter now and there was no time to listen to eulogies for Scarpino. There were three to go, Baron last.

"A fresh grave without a marker," Tony Quince went on. "You know what I'm going to do? In a month, two months, three months, some guys are going to come in here in the middle of the night and put up a stone. Scarpino, with his name and when he was born and when he kicked. To make it official."

I watched Tony's face. He wanted to laugh out loud but he just couldn't bring it off. He'd been planning this, setting it up, but now he couldn't laugh over it. Later, maybe. Not yet.

One at a time we walked over to the car and got in. Nobody said anything. It was real now, real all the way. This wasn't a movie, and there was no turning back, not with Scarpino in the hole and the dirt falling on him.

That was part of it.

The rest was identification. An obvious identification, one our minds couldn't miss. A strong identification with Scarpino, and a fairly good understanding of what it was like to face a gun and know it was going to blow your head off in a minute or two. A picture of Scarpino in his grave and a far more frightening picture of ourselves in graves of our own.

Angie started the car and headed for the rooming house where Johnny Carr and Leon Spiro lived.

We left the car around the corner. We walked to an old rooming house with rocking chairs on the porch. Once it had been a private home, somebody's mansion. I don't think they had painted it since then and that had been a long time ago. The front door was locked. Angie took a long-bladed knife from his pocket and opened the door. We trooped inside.

Somewhere somebody was taking a shower. The sounds of the plumbing carried through the large old house. Someone somewhere else was cooking something and the smells got around as well as the plumbing noises. Tony said, "Two flights up." We followed him.

There was a threadbare carpet on the stairs for one flight, then just bare wood. Both sets of stairs creaked magnificently. On the second floor a door opened and a haggard woman shuffled down the hall to the community bathroom. She looked like a superannuated whore. The third floor was empty and silent. Tony paused for a minute to find his bearings. Then he pointed to one of four identical wooden doors.

We walked to it. Angie had his knife out. He tried the door. It wasn't locked and he eased it open slowly, gently. It whined at us but quietly.

We stepped inside. Tony was the last in and he closed the door. This time it didn't make a sound. The room was dark, all the shades drawn and no lights on. It took my eyes a while to get used to the darkness. Then I could see—for what it was worth.

There was one big double bed in the room with all three of them in it. The bedclothing was in a heap on the floor at the foot of the bed. The girl was in the middle, sprawled on her back, her dirty blond hair spread over a pillow. Mustache lay on her right with his face buried in the crook of her neck and his arm draped across her just below her large breasts. Johnny was curled up on the other side of the girl with his feet alongside her face and his head resting upon her thigh.

I looked at the three of them and felt my stomach go tight. I pictured the three of them, two cheap punks and their girl, spending every night finding new ways for three people to turn each other on. The room was filled with the overpowering odor of stale sex and pot.

"Pigs," Angie said. "A bunch of pigs that stink."

The girl shifted slightly in her sleep. Her red mouth was puffy from sleep and sex. Her waist was thick and in repose her flesh looked soft and flabby. She had prominent veins in her legs and a dark bluish bruise high on one thigh.

Tony had a gun in his hand. I wondered how he could use it in a rooming house full of people. Then I looked at Angie and saw the long sharp knife.

Angie was very good with the knife. He took Johnny first, slipping the thin blade into his back between the ribs and into the heart. Johnny died without opening his eyes, without moving his head from the girl's thigh. When Angie withdrew the knife there was hardly any blood at all.

He got Mustache the same way but when the blade sank home Mustache went just a little tense and his face moved against the girl's throat.

Just enough to wake her.

She yawned and stretched. Her puffed lips curled in a sensual smile. She yawned again and rolled over onto her side toward Johnny. Her thighs fastened around his head and her mouth sought him in greedy hunger.

Then she opened her eyes.

And saw us.

She said, "Angie? Tony? I don't—"

"You had to wake up," Angie said. "You dumb horny pig of a broad, you slut, you never get enough, you had to wake up ready for more. You couldn't sleep just a minute more, no. You had to wake up."

When she saw the knife her eyes went wide in terror and her mouth opened for a scream. She never got it out. Angie clapped a hand over her mouth and drew the knife across her throat, slashing it all the way open. The blood bubbled out of her like water from a broken sewer main. When it stopped he took his hand from her mouth and wiped blood and prints from the knife with one of the bedsheets. His face was a blend of green and gray. He stuck the knife between the girl's legs and left it there.

"That stupid pig," he kept saying. "That stupid, stupid pig."

We got out at Tony's house, sent Angie home and switched to Tony's car. We sat in the front seat and smoked cigarettes. I tried to guess how long I had been without sleep. A long time and it felt longer. Too many people had died.

And one was left.

"The tough one," Tony said. "The big one, Nat. The others were practice, something that had to happen. Lou Baron is different. If we don't get him and get him right, then the rest was a mistake. This is the big one."

I asked him if we could stop for coffee. Lou couldn't know anything yet, not this early, not from Scarpino, not from Johnny and Mustache, not from Philly. Tony found a diner and we sat at the counter. A waitress who looked as tired as I felt served us very hot coffee in heavy china mugs. It was bitter but I didn't complain.

"There's somebody that lives with Lou, You know who?"

"Porky."

"That's the one," he said. "So he's on the list too. Porky looks slow but isn't, Nat. Lou makes him look like a servant. Porky's more than that. He can play with a knife or a gun or those big hands he's got. He was on a chain gang in Georgia, got in a fight with another con and broke the other guy's back over his knee. He has a gun on all the time."

I finished my coffee and motioned for more. By the time she brought me a fresh cup Tony was ready for a refill. The coffee helped a lot. The tiredness had made me numb and slowed me down. The coffee was taking the edge of fatigue away.

"I'm not afraid of a gunshot," Tony said. "His house is pretty quiet. A gun goes off in there, nobody hears it. In that neighborhood they don't run for the cops anyway."

"Anybody else live there? Aside from Baron and Porky?"

"Just the two of them."

"Then I'll go alone."

He stared at me. "You nuts?"

"I'm serious. He's expecting me. I'm back from a job in Philly and I had something to tell him. There was more there than he told me about, remember? He gave me a wrong make on the job. So maybe there was some kind of a snag and I have to tell him about it."

Tony was interested.

I said, "It makes sense, Tony. If he sees you it's a battle because he must know you're thinking about a move. If I come, all alone…"

"Yeah."

"You like it?"

"I like it, Nat. You got nerve, you know?"

I let that one go by. "All alone," I said. "You can take me back to the Stennett. I'll pick up my car and go it alone. He'll see nothing but me in my car coming to report to him."

"It's pretty, Nat. I like it."

"Hell," I said. "I think I'll call Baron. Then we'll see how he feels about it."

13

I called Lou Baron from a diner. The phone was on the wall in the rear and I leaned against the wall while I dialed his number. It rang for a while. Then Baron answered it.

"Nat, Lou."

"You in town?"

"I just got in."

"Something go wrong?" Baron asked.

I made myself hesitate. "It's hard to say," I said finally. "A long story. Can I come over?"

"Now?"

"If it's okay."

"Sure," he said. "Come on over, Nat. I'll be waiting for you."

The last line bothered me a little. I put the receiver on the hook and got a new cigarette going. My lungs were smoke-stale and my eyes weren't focusing just right. I went back to the counter to swallow more coffee. Then Tony dropped me off at the Stennett and I picked up my car.

I left the top up on the Lincoln. I drove slowly, my hands easy on the wheel, the gun tucked comfortably under the waistband of my trousers. I was the angel of death with chrome wings and no halo. I was hell in a short-brimmed hat.

Sunlight kept getting in my eyes. I found Baron's house and parked my car in front of it. I looked at my watch but I didn't even notice the time. Just looking at the watch was enough. A present, *To Nat from Lou Baron*.

Ah, the hell with it. Baron wasn't my brother. We didn't go to school together. Two months ago I didn't even know he was

alive. The watch was payment for a competent job of professional beating, not a token of love and friendship. He was a
hood and I was a hood and you can't make high drama out of
one hood blowing the head off of another hood. Shakespeare
managed it but that was another story. And Brutus wasn't exactly
a hood anyway. More a misguided nut.

So the hell with it.

Porky answered the door. "Crowley," I said. "I think he's expecting me."

Porky didn't say anything. He never did—maybe he didn't
know how to talk. I looked at him more closely than usual and
noticed the way his jacket bulged a little in front on the left
side. Tony was right. Porky still packed a gun.

We made the usual promenade together—through the hallway
to the living room. Baron was sitting in his chair. He was wearing
a bathrobe this time around, a rich maroon affair. He had deer-
skin slippers on his feet and a cup of coffee in one hand.

Porky crossed the room and disappeared. I didn't sit down. I
looked at Baron—he must have been sleeping when I called
and he was still in the process of waking up. "Trouble, Nat?"

"Not exactly. I made the flight, met the finger. A tub of lard
named Jack Garstein."

"I don't know him."

The power was still there. The eyes were calm, the hands
steady. He was waiting to hear what I had to say. But first I had
to get Porky into the room. I asked Baron if I could get myself a
cup of coffee.

"Stay here," he said. "Porky'll get it." He yelled for Porky, told
him to bring me a cup of coffee. While we waited I killed time
playing with a cigarette. I shook out the match and found an
ashtray to put it into. Then Porky came back.

Porky had a saucer in one hand with a china cup balanced on

it. Steam came up from the brim of the cup. In his other hand he had a silver tray holding a creamer and a sugar bowl. There was a gun under his jacket but he never had a chance to move near it.

My gun was tucked under my belt. I took it out, aimed, squeezed the trigger. I shot Porky in the chest, maybe an inch or two north of the heart. He took two steps and died. The coffee went all over the rug. So did the cream and sugar. But by then the gun was pointed at Baron.

"Why, Nat?"

I didn't have an answer handy. I stood there, the gun pointed at him, and he sat where he was, his eyes on me, not the gun. He didn't move at all. He may have been nervous but none of it showed. His question was a real one. He wanted to know why.

"Because you're through," I said.

"Who's behind it?"

"Tony Quince."

Baron nodded thoughtfully. "All right," he said. "It figures. He's well connected, he's hungry. I suppose I should have been ready for it—and from him. But not this soon. You didn't go to Philly, Nat, did you?"

"I went. I shot the finger and came home."

"And now you shoot me."

"That's right," I said.

He thought it over for a few seconds. He still wasn't nervous. He was a fast hard man looking for an opening.

"Don't kill me, Nat."

He didn't whimper it. He said it calmly, sensibly. He made me want to put the gun away, sit down, have a drink. I told him I had no choice.

"Don't shoot me," Baron said again. "Do a turn, change sides. We'll clean up Tony and a few boys in no time and you'll be on the right team."

Everybody was telling me which side to play. "Your team's gone," I said. "Dead."

"How many?"

"Scarpino and Spiro and Carr. And Porky here."

"Four," he said. "Four I never needed in the first place. Let me live, Nat."

"No."

I should have shot him then and saved time. For some reason I didn't. I wasn't sure why. I held the gun and kept it on him. He stayed where he was and looked at me.

He said, "I made a mistake. I guessed wrong. I thought you were just looking for a couple of yards a week, an inside track, a soft touch. I didn't know how much you wanted."

"I don't want much."

"I would've given you more, Nat. I just wanted to put you where you wanted to be, that's all. Quince put me wise about you, told me you were around. I heard a little from other people but he gave me a name and a little background. He said I could do worse than find a slot for you. Were you in his pocket all along?"

That was a hard one to answer. I wasn't too sure myself.

"He brought you in," he said. "He brought you in all on his own, set you up with me. That it?"

"No."

"You were running from something. You—ah, the hell with it. I don't know about you and I don't care about you. I played it straight with you, Crowley. I gave you more than I had to give you."

"Let's say we used each other."

"So? Who gets more than that out of anybody?"

I let that one go.

"I got time for a cigar?" Baron asked.

"No."

"Then end it, Crowley."

The gun was cocked and ready. A Smith and Wesson thirty-eight primed and ready to go. The gun worked beautifully. It had one notch coming already. Porky was lying in his own blood at our feet and we were both ignoring him.

I said, "There's something I want to say."

"Then say it. You got the gun."

"You had me wrong all the way, Lou."

"That's something new?"

"Wrong all the way and more than you know. My name's not Crowley."

"Who cares?"

"My name's Donald Barshter," I said. "I had a gun in my hand in Korea, never before and never since. Until I hit Buffalo I lived in Connecticut and I sold insurance. I was married and lived in a little house with trees in front of it."

"Huh?"

"I was a square. Then I killed my wife by mistake and ran. I decided to play mobster. And here I am. I faked everybody out, Lou. I'm a phony all through."

"You're full of crap."

"You think so?"

He stared thoughtfully at me. "Maybe not," he said. "God damn. You put on a good act, Crowley. But I don't get it. Why tell me all this?"

I wasn't too sure myself.

I steadied the gun. "It won't do you any good," I said. "You're not going to run around shouting about it. And I had to tell somebody."

We could have talked about it for another five days the way we were going. But it wouldn't have made much sense. I shot

Baron once in the face, wiped off the gun and tossed it in his lap. Then I got the hell out of there and drove the Lincoln back to the Stennett.

I called Tony.

"It's over," I said.

"It worked?"

"I'm talking to you. If it hadn't worked…"

"Yeah," he said. "I know."

"So tell people," I said. "Do whatever you want to do. I'm going to bed, I'm beat."

And I went to bed.

From there on it was Tony Quince's ball and he ran with it. The routine was what he called it, a palace revolution with the organization staying intact and just the very top turning around. He had spent the last three months laying the groundwork and it couldn't have run more smoothly. There were no more killings. A few men who had been fairly close to Baron left town in a hurry. Nobody went chasing after them. They weren't that important.

A few others found themselves with a little less responsibility and a little less money. A bookie had his area cut down. Another man had one of his three after-hours' joints taken from him and handed to somebody else. You didn't need a bloodbath for this. Just quiet conversation, backed up with power—power held carefully in reserve.

Somebody found Johnny and Mustache and their community-property female in the rooming house that afternoon, and that one made the papers. The story was about as colorful as you could get—a trio, so nude and so dead, after an obviously hectic evening of fun and games. A *ménage à trois* if there ever was one. The newspapers called it a sex killing and the cops were too tired to argue. There was never a kick on that one.

Scarpino never got found. The gravediggers covered him up and put grass in place over him and that was it for Scarpino. There were conflicting rumors, the way there always are—some people said he left town on the run, others that he was weighted down in the middle of Lake Erie. Nobody much missed him, except maybe his father. And his father wasn't talking.

Baron was something else.

The cops picked us up Tuesday night and hauled us in—Tony Quince and Angie Moscato and me. The cops were the same pair of bulls who had pulled me in the first time around, a Fred Zeigler and a Howard Kardaman. This time I didn't get slapped at all. There was no booking, no hard wordplay. They were being very cagy—if we were going to run things in Buffalo, they didn't want to rub us the wrong way. As far as evidence went, they knew better than to look for any. They knew we had alibis and that we wouldn't leave calling cards on dead bodies. They put Baron and Porky on adjoining slabs at the morgue and didn't worry about them.

By Wednesday even the police realized that Tony Quince had the city in his pocket. Patrolmen started nodding respectfully at me when I walked down the street. Zeigler and Kardaman wrote Baron and Porky off as jobs done by person or persons unknown. And the newspapers had fun with it. It was the biggest story since McKinley got his.

They called it a Mafia job, performed by syndicate hoodlums under the direction of the all-powerful Unione Siciliano. They made Baron an ancient henchman of Dutch Schultz, with connections with Touhy, and explained that he'd been assassinated by remnants of the old Capone mob. It was a brilliant job of theorizing and the only thing I could find wrong with it was that it had no basis in fact. But you can't expect much more from newspapermen. Their sourcebook on crime is a mass of printed matter on the topic, all of it written by other newsmen. They make the myths and wind up believing them.

So I spent a week sitting around the apartment, sometimes with a bottle handy, sometimes without. I took Annie out for dinner twice and wound up in bed with her once—at my place, the Stennett.

It was brutal sex, murderous sex.

Because I was a murderer now. Not just a killer, a man who'd accidentally knocked his wife's head in, a man who'd once been to war. I'd looked men in the eyes now, men who begged me for their lives, and I'd taken their lives instead. I'd felt my finger tighten on the trigger. I'd sent bullets into their bodies. And I made love now like I was sending bullets into Anne's.

But Anne, who knew damn well what I'd done even though I hadn't told her and she hadn't asked, performed as if she were a killer too—between the stretches where she acted as if she were my victim.

Both roles had rubbed off on her, the killer's and the victim's. Because I was murderer and victim both. Anybody who kills is his own victim—each time you kill you destroy something of yourself.

And in the sex with Anne I was destroying some of my own sensitivity—Barshter's or Crowley's, it didn't matter which.

I had never had sex like this before, sex that went on and on until Anne begged me to finish her off, bring her to climax for God's sake.

But I wouldn't bring her to climax. I stretched out the act to the point of the sadistic, so that Anne finally had to finish herself off. And I wouldn't let her alone even after she did that—I kept on going, starting her off again on the ascent toward orgasm. She tried to wrench herself away from me but I wouldn't have that. I pinioned her and stroked her until she was a twitching mass of sensation—and then I abruptly stopped and she had to finish herself again while I watched. And I did watch, my breath coming hard, well past my limits but not done, as if there was a hole inside me deeper than the hole we put Scarpino in, and I'd been shoveling as hard as I could but it just wouldn't get filled.

Anne tormented me in retaliation, abruptly stopping when I was finally on the verge and laughing while I tried to bring myself to gratification. In a fury I hit her and she sank her teeth into the soft flesh near my armpit and closed her fist like a vise around my main male armament.

I slapped her face but she wouldn't let go.

"Cool it," I said.

"No," Anne said.

"You're a bitch," I said.

"And what kind of name do they call you, Nat? Maybe you have no name at all. Maybe what I'm holding onto is anonymous—it could belong to anybody." She squeezed mercilessly.

I slapped her again, harder, and this time she let go. I fell on her and she flexed her legs and she screamed and took me inside her.

Both of us rocked and plunged. We slammed at each other as if we were out for blood. We reeked with sweat and started sliding all over each other. It was a savage act, a killer's act—but neither of us died. Only parts of us died. Parts of our humanity died.

What was left was the inhumanity. I plundered Anne's breasts until she sobbed. I dug at her until there was blood, real blood, not something I saw in a nightmare. And she again used her teeth on me until I saw red and I chopped at her ruthlessly.

We acted like a couple of stone-age animals. Like a couple of dervishes whirling to sacrifice each other.

We were exhausted, finally, and we fell asleep. When I awoke, Anne was gone, back to her own place, I guessed. It was morning and I went out to breakfast. Without Anne it was a quiet time.

Which was good, because I didn't feel much like noise. I'd had noise enough for a lifetime, the sort you hear and the sort you feel in every nerve ending. There had been Garstein in Philadelphia, then Johnny and Mustache and Porky and Scarpino and Baron. And the girl, the girl whose name I had never bothered to find out, the hard little blonde who had picked the wrong time to wake up and who had died for it. The girl who had been killed as an afterthought.

Seven of them, if you bothered keeping score. Three of them were mine—Garstein and Baron and Porky. The rest were Angie's but I had watched them die.

It was more blood than I was used to—outside of a movie screen. And this was the sort that doesn't vanish when the lights come up.

14

As I said, things had changed at the top, and I had an office now on the eighteenth floor of a downtown office building. I had a free-form desk, a few soft chairs, a Modigliani reproduction on the wall and a taut-hipped redhead who answered the phone when it rang and typed things now and then. The redhead was somebody's sister and the job was a soft touch for her—she spent most of her time either talking to her girlfriends on the phone or polishing her nails. She didn't even have to put out for the boss, although I'd thought about giving her a tumble. But she was somebody's sister and it wasn't good form to fool around with someone's sister even if you outranked him. Besides, I had enough going between Annie and Brenda. I might try the redhead on sooner or later, the way you try on any stray female who looks as though she might be fairly good at it, like an occasional hooker from one of our downtown houses, an occasional stripper from one of our nightclubs—and all of them more than happy to do it for free, because I was Nat Crowley. But for now I had my fill, and so far I'd let the redhead alone. She didn't exactly know what I did in my office, only that she was supposed to keep her mouth shut. Whenever somebody important came around I sent her out for coffee. That's where she was now.

Tony said, "You could have more interests, Nat."

"I've got enough."

"If you say so. You could meet people, do more things, make more dough. This way you just sit around and handle bookkeeping. That's a job for a goddamn accountant."

It was more than that but I didn't bother saying so. Tony knew it anyway. I had my office and I handled all the paperwork that had to be handled. I kept the two sets of books—one for us and another for the government—and I made sure that both sets balanced neatly. I made sure that the right amount of dough was coming in from our various income properties and that not too much was getting siphoned off into private pockets. I looked at the bills and wrote the checks. We had a lot of things going for us and there were a lot of bills to pay and a lot of records to check.

The income came from three sources. There was the legitimate stuff, which took care of a big portion of our revenue. We ran jukeboxes and vending machines and a lot of local trucking. We owned a few construction outfits and a batch of nightclubs and smaller taverns. The ownership may have started because we used muscle a long time ago but now the whole routine was puritanically straight.

Then there were the rackets, everything from dope to dirty pictures, and we had a little of everything in those departments. They were illegal but they had to be run the same way as a legitimate business. The same rules applied—supply and demand, profit and loss, income and expenditures.

The third class was investments. You could buy a piece of a stock swindle or a satchel of hot money or anything else. You invested your dough and took a capital gain or loss the way Wall Street plays the market or the way Swiss bankers bet on Latin American revolutions. We had a lot going for us there, too, and I kept busy.

"There are people to meet," Tony said. "You've got a little dough—you could get something going on your own. Open a club, start a business. The dough is there. All you got to do is take it."

"I'm happy."

"You sure?"

"Positive. I like to sit in the background, Tony. It's quieter."

"You hot?"

I shook my head. "I just hate flashbulbs. They hurt my eyes."

"You must be hotter than hell," he said. "What's the charge?"

"No charge."

"Nothing that can get fixed?"

He couldn't fix murder in Connecticut. And that would be the charge if they started printing my picture in the papers. The captions didn't have to call me a hood. They could refer to me as a captain of local industry and the payoff would still be the same. A trip to Connecticut and the end of the ballgame.

"Nothing you can fix," I said.

Tony walked over to the window and looked out. He asked me if I had anything to drink. I kept a bottle of the red wine he liked in a desk drawer. I poured him a glass and he sipped it.

"You been working hard, Nat."

"Not too hard."

"It's September," he said. "You worked all summer without a break. I took a few weeks, went up in Canada to catch fish. Everybody takes a vacation in the summer. Even the slobs who work for a living get away for a week in the mountains. You stayed cooped up in a lousy little office…"

"It's a good office. And I'm here a hot three days a week."

"Still, you need a vacation."

I didn't say anything. I took out a cigarette and lit it with my lighter. The lighter was fourteen-karat gold and it worked perfectly. It was engraved, *To Nat From Tony.*

"Ever been to Vegas?" Tony asked.

"Not for a while."

"You're not hot there, are you?"

"I told you," I said. "I'm not hot at all. Anywhere."

"Sure," he said. "I forgot. Vegas is a nice town, Nat. You'd like it there for a week. Everything on the company, of course. A paid vacation. Stay at a good hotel, eat good food and drink good liquor."

"You mean there's a job for me?"

He shook his head. "Strictly a vacation," he said. "Oh, there's a guy or two you should see. Just to talk to. It's good to keep in touch with people, good for business. But I could send anybody down. Hell, I could go myself. I just think you could use a vacation."

"Maybe I could."

"Stay a week or two weeks. Put up at the High Rise. It's a good place and I know the guy who runs it, guy name of Dan Gordon. A sweet guy—you'll like him. When can you leave?"

"Any time."

"I'll call Gordon," he said. "Tell him to have the red carpet ready. You want me to tell him to keep a broad on ice for you? Or do you want to bring your own?"

I put out my cigarette. "I'll bring my own," I said.

I saw Anne that night. I picked her up and we ran over to our favorite place for steaks and then drove out along the lakeshore. There was a summer-stock outfit out there and they were doing an Arthur Miller thing that she wanted to see. The meal was good, the drive cool and fresh, the play not too bad. It was a tight gutty script and even a bunch of amateurs couldn't louse it up too badly. Annie enjoyed it.

The relationship we'd managed to drift into was a kind of cockeyed one. We didn't talk about that night we'd had, after the killings. We hadn't forgotten it—we just didn't talk about it. It hung there between us, a violent moment I think neither of us wanted to face squarely. Instead, we kept things on the surface. We saw each other two, three times a week. I rarely called her. I would run into her at one of the spots she frequented or, occasionally, pick her up at the club where she worked. She waited tables there a few nights a week. It was a sucker trap. The pay was a joke but tips were good and she made enough to cover the rent on her apartment.

We ate together some of the time, saw a show together some of the time, drove around together some of the time, slept together some of the time.

So far as I knew, Anne wasn't seeing anybody else.

Still, we weren't going together exactly. We had no claims on each other, no strings to pull. She was pretty familiar with my apartment at the Stennett, but she still lived in her own humble flat and spent most of her nights with no bedroom company. It was loose and uncommitted, the rules not too well defined.

On the way back from the summer playhouse I had the Lincoln's top down. The wind played with Anne's hair. The air was cool and clearer than usual. The moon wasn't around but there were a hell of a lot of stars in the sky. I draped an arm around her and she leaned against it.

"Good play," I said.

"What would a hood like you know about plays?"

"I'm a very dramatic hood."

"Uh-huh." She had her head cocked and she was looking at me in a special way she had—sizing me up, trying to look through me. It was a habit of hers. Sometimes it bothered me a little.

"A dramatic hood," she said. "Too dramatic. You play games with words, Nat."

"Meaning?"

"I don't know. Where did you go to college?"

"Tuskegee Institute," I said. "I'm passing."

"Uh-huh. You're an odd one, Nat."

We always fenced verbally. Sometimes I thought of it as a rather involved form of foreplay. It wasn't just that, though. And it was less fencing than wrestling. We used words like half-nelsons.

I said, "I'm just an organization man, ma'am."

"The hood in the gray flannel suit?"

"Uh-huh. The modern mobster. It's all a business now—haven't you heard? You need a college diploma to rob a filling station. That's what happens when you get mass education and automation going for you."

"Did you explain all that to Baron when you shot him?"

She said it casually, but it was like a casual stroke with a shiv.

"I read about that," I said. "The Mafia murdered him. It said so in the papers."

"And all you know—"

"—is what I read in the papers. Put your head down, Annie. Relax."

She put her head down. I can't say she relaxed. I took the skyway into the city, then drove around aimlessly for a while. We stopped somewhere on the north side and had a drink in a quiet neighborhood bar. There was an old Bogart movie on the television set but the picture kept rolling and the bartender kept trying to fix it. We left.

Back in the car again I said, "I'm taking a vacation. A week or two in Las Vegas. Why don't you come along for the ride?"

She thought it over. "I don't want to," she said.

"Why not?"

"Reasons."

"It would be a break. A lot of sun, a comfortable hotel suite, a different floor show every night. Fifty different ways to lose money legally. All-expense-paid vacation for two. How about it?"

"Thanks but no."

"Why not?"

She asked me for a cigarette. I took out two, lit them both and gave one to her. She smoked half of it before she said anything. "Because I don't want to be kept."

"Huh?"

"I'm independent. I live in a dump. Not because I have a big romantic love for dumps or for wearing a dress too many times or for working. But because it's better that way. It would be easy to let you pay all the bills, Nat. Move in on you, let you take care of rent and clothes and everything else."

She finished the cigarette and threw it out of the car. "Then you'd own me," she went on. "Then you'd have that hold, that upper hand. And I don't want that."

"So pay your own way."

"I can't afford it. I'm just a working girl."

I didn't exactly get it. "I'm not hiring you as a slave girl. I'm just selling you a free trip to Las Vegas."

"I'm sorry," she said. "But it's no sale, Nat."

I got mad. "Do you really think you can say no to me anymore? In this town?"

She shook her head. "Because you're such a big man now, is that it? Have you forgotten what you were when I first met you, Nat? Other people might not remember, but I do. No," she said, "it's not hard to say no to you, Nat. You make it easy."

She was wrong.

I didn't sleep with her that night. I went upstairs to her apartment and we had a few drinks. Then we called it a night. I left her there, went back to my car and drove back to the Stennett. I put the car away and elevated to my own apartment. It was a pretty impressive place now. Not too long after Baron's death I had had the management get rid of their furniture and replaced it with furniture of my own. I had gone to one of the better furniture stores and picked out French Provincial pieces, expensive but worth it. The place made a good show when we had important people in from out of town and it was comfortable when I was there by myself. The hotel-room feeling was gone.

I got a bottle of rye from the bar and poured myself a drink. I stirred it with a silver stirrer and drank most of it in a few minutes.

Then I got on the phone.

I called the club where Anne worked and asked for Lundgren, the skinny Swede who managed it. It took them a few minutes to find him. Then he said hello to me.

I said, "Annie Bishop works for you. Right?"

"That's right, Mr. Crowley."

"Yeah. Well she doesn't work there anymore."

"She's quitting?"

"She's quitting. When she comes in, you tell her she's quitting. You understand?"

He understood. I hung up while he was still trying to tell me how glad he was to do me a favor. I called Noomie's.

"If Anne Bishop comes in," I said, "she doesn't get served."

They didn't ask why. It was an order and their business consisted in part in obeying orders from certain people. I was one of those people. They assured me she wouldn't be served.

I put down the phone and finished my drink. I lit a cigarette and wondered why I was going to all this trouble just to take a girl to Las Vegas. It would have been easy enough to find some other broad who was tickled to go. It would have been even easier to tell Tony that Gordon should arrange a girl for me. They have pretty girls in Las Vegas, obliging girls, friendly girls. Girls who don't go for verbal wrestling matches but keep their wrestling on a purely physical plane.

So why all this trouble for Annie Bishop?

Hell, she had it figured right. It was all a business of holds, of getting the upper hand. That was the way she saw it, the way she played it. That was the code of the jungle, or whatever the hell you want to call it. So that was the way it would go.

I picked up the phone book again and thumbed through it. I put in a call to a man named Hankin. He was a slum landlord with tenement property all over town. He happened to own a few run-down buildings on the street Anne lived on. Including hers.

"Nat Crowley," I said. "You busy?"

He'd been sleeping and he still wasn't exactly awake. But I was Nat Crowley and he had to be nice to me if he were going to stay in business. He had tenements with too many violations in them. We fixed these things for him, and he was nice to us.

"What can I do for you, Nat?"

"About one of those rockpiles of yours," I said. I gave him the address. "Do the tenants have leases?"

"No," he said. "I don't like leases."

He didn't like leases or rent control or lots of things. I said, "There's a tenant of yours who ought to get evicted. Anne Bishop."

"I know who you mean. She pays her rent first of every month, like a clock."

"Call her in the morning and tell her to move out within a week. Can you do that?"

"She pays by the month, Nat. So she's paid up through the first of October. But I can tell her to get out by then."

"Do that," I said.

"Sure, Nat. Anything I can do—"

"I appreciate it."

I hung up on him and built myself a fresh drink. Then I went back to the phone and made a few more calls.

✴

It took three days.

She called me at the Stennett. It was around noon and I was asleep when the phone rang. I yawned, lit a cigarette, answered it.

"You're a son of a bitch, Nat," Anne said.

I laughed softly.

"A real son of a bitch. Why didn't you have a few goons come over and beat me up? Or something subtle, like acid in the face?"

"I like your face."

"Uh-huh. All of a sudden I don't have a job. All of a sudden I don't have a roof over my head. All of a sudden I can't even buy a drink in this goddamned town. Isn't that cute?"

I dragged on my cigarette. "It sounds rough."

"Doesn't it? You don't issue invitations, Nat. You issue ultimatums. I don't like ultimatums."

I didn't say anything. I smoked my cigarette and let her dangle on her end of the phone.

"No place to live, no job, nothing to do. What am I supposed to do, Nat?"

"You should leave town."

"Should I?"

"Sure. You should come to Las Vegas. With me."

A pause. "An ultimatum, Nat?"

"Call it an invitation."

Another pause, followed by a question: "When, Nat?"

"Pack. I'll call the airport."

15

We had a nonstop jet complete with pretty hostesses, a silken takeoff and a featherbed landing. Somebody's hireling met us at the airport and drove us to the High Rise in a Cadillac that was still shining. Everybody drove Cadillacs in Las Vegas. They weren't even status symbols. Just union cards.

The High Rise was one of the big ones—a lot of glitter, a lot of lushness, big names for entertainment and roulette wheels that never quit turning. The manager called me by name and gave me a heavy handshake. He helped me sign in while a sharp-eyed kid went away with our bags. The manager took us to our suite all by himself. It was on the fifth floor and it was big. There was a private bar stocked with liquor and a private slot so I could throw away quarters without getting out of bed. He said he hoped everything was all right. I wondered if I were supposed to tip him but he went away before I could give the problem too much thought.

I opened a suitcase and started hanging things in a closet. Without saying anything, Annie went over to the bar and I heard ice clinking. She came over and handed me a glass of rye and soda. She had gin and tonic. We touched glasses and drank.

"You're all right," I said. "Every room should come with an in-house cocktail waitress."

"Maybe they all do."

"Something wrong?"

Her eyes were hard to read. "Nothing," she said. "I'm just dazzled. The VIP treatment is a new one."

"You'll get used to it."

"Will I? How long did it take you to get used to it, Nat?"

"Not too long."

"Not long at all. And how long did it take you to get used to murder, Nat?" My eyes hardened, but she went on. "Was that hard to do? Or did it come easy? Did you find you liked it…?"

I finished my drink and put the glass down on a table. I looked at her and she stopped talking. There was anger in her eyes now, anger and contempt and maybe a little fear.

"You shouldn't talk about things you know nothing about," I said. "You're in no position to talk."

"I'm not?"

"You're not. You know how we're registered at this hotel? Not Mr. and Mrs. Just plain Nathaniel Crowley. You don't count at all, honey. You're just part of the luggage."

I was sorry the minute I said it. I should have apologized but I didn't. I got out of my clothes and took a shower.

I met Dan Gordon after dinner that night. He came over to our table while we were being bored by the floor show, introduced himself, stuck out a sweaty hand and then sat down with us. He had a platinum chorus-line pony with him. She had good legs, big breasts and a blandly bovine face. She didn't say anything. I had the feeling, just from spending some time at the same table with her, that it was better that way. She was purely decorative.

"I heard a lot about you," Gordon told me. "Tony and I are tight for years. He says you're a big help to him."

"We get along."

He laughed loudly and too long. "I guess you do," he said. "Tony says you're in town a week, two weeks. He says make you happy, show you a big time. My boys treating you all right, Nat?"

"Everything's fine," I said. "This is quite a place."

"You like it?"

I nodded. I didn't—it was a little too goddamn glittery. But I didn't want to hurt his feelings.

"We try to give the customer his money's worth," he was saying. "We run a hell of a place. Can't find a better place in the whole damned town, and this is a hell of a town. Right, Pigeon?"

Pigeon was the pony. She sat there for a minute trying to figure out what was supposed to be right, then gave a half-hearted nod. He patted her on one of her pretty knees and told me what a great kid she was.

"A hell of a town," he said again. "You meet my manager? Smoothest guy going. Went to hotel management school up at Cornell, then ran a summer place on Cape Cod for a year. I was up there, happened to see the job he was doing, offered him full-time here. I pay big dough. He couldn't afford to turn me down. He does a hell of a job."

"Fine service," I said. I had to say something.

"You said it. And we don't make a dime on the hotel, Nat. Our money comes right out of the casino—the tables, the wheels, the cards, the slots. The hotel is charity."

A pretty waitress came by with fresh drinks. Gordon pinched her and she smiled benignly at him. On the stage, a strip act had given way to a comic telling sick jokes. He had a reputation for hysterical hip cynicism, and the unconscious comedy of the Las Vegas audience inspired him to greater heights. He was very unpleasant, very sick and very funny. I missed most of the punch lines because Gordon talked too much.

"Vegas," Gordon said reverently. "First you make it legal. Then you keep it honest. Then you wrap it up nice and put a pretty ribbon around it, so it's a vacation instead of a chance to roll dice. And you watch the money come in. It just keeps on coming."

I lit a fresh cigarette and wished he would go away.

"What kind of action you like, Nat?"

"I don't gamble much."

He guffawed. That was one of his favorite tricks. "Not much of a gambler, huh?"

"I don't like to take chances."

Another guffaw. "Sure," he said. "You like sure things, huh? You like a little edge. You're all right, Nat."

There was more of this. Finally he found other things to do. He left, taking his platinum pony with him. The comic finished up and went away. We tried the casino. I wasted a few dollars on craps while Annie went away to worry one of the slots to death. The crap table bored me. I took Annie away from the machine and we went upstairs.

It was restful, anyway.

The High Rise pool was a sort of lake with a concrete bottom. It was nicely surrounded by deck chairs, with or without sun umbrellas, and each deck chair had a little round white table beside it. That was where your waiter put your drinks.

We had deck chairs without umbrellas. I wanted a suntan and Annie didn't seem to care too much one way or the other. We spent three days doing very little outside of soaking up sunlight. The sun was one of Las Vegas's constants—every day, from six in the morning until six at night, the sun was undeniably there. The clouds never got in its way. The sun sat up there, burning, and I let it darken my skin. Every once in a while I would go loll in the pool. I couldn't swim worth a damn, but nobody at the High Rise did much swimming. The pool was something to be in between drinks, between gambling, between sex and liquor. I would lower myself into water always the right temperature, walk around, paddle around, float on my back like a corpse. Then, when it got monotonous, I would clamber out of the pool and let the sun bake me some more.

We spent our nights gambling or being entertained, or both. There were a pair of meets with people Tony had wanted me to see, silly affairs where we sat around in a private room sipping whiskey and talking amiably, if guardedly. We didn't deal in specifics. It all had its point and I could see the point easily enough. Tony was a man with friends, but he wasn't that firmly established. He had taken over from Baron, had killed Baron to do it. So we had to be nice to people, had to firm up friendships here and there. I was a sort of gangland liaison man, Tony's personal ambassador to the world.

Annie and I maintained relations that were generally cordial, sometimes almost warm, occasionally chilly. She was moody a lot of the time. She let herself drift away from the world and sat for hours listening to music on the radio or reading from any of several slim books of poems. I picked up one of the poetry books when she was busy in the can. The stuff was harsh and dry. The images were vivid but the taste of it all was as acrid as marijuana smoke.

Sometimes I wondered why I had brought Anne along. Before this there had been something of a special quality to our relationship, something that made it a little more than the usual story of a hood and his girl, and that quality was gone now. I had killed it.

The worst part was that I had screwed up the thing we had had between us and I didn't even want what I had gained. For three days and three nights I didn't touch her. I owned her, she belonged to me and I could have had her any way I wanted her. But I wound up not wanting her at all. I couldn't figure it out.

There were two double beds in the room. She slept in hers and I slept in mine. And that was the way it was. She would give me funny looks at bedtime, looks that asked whether I wanted her or not, and I would pretend I didn't notice the looks and would mumble something about how tired I was. Then I would go to bed and toss for a few hours, wanting her but not wanting her, needing the release she could bring me but unable to go over there and take it.

The third night we went up to the room together and I made drinks for both of us. I sat in a cushy chair and worked on my drink. She put hers down on a table and took off all her clothes. She usually undressed methodically, putting everything neatly away in turn. Now she let her clothes pile up on the floor.

"Look, Nat," she said.

I looked. She had as chokingly lovely a body as I had ever seen. She wasn't big enough in breast or butt to make a *Playboy* foldout, but there was something about the soft sweet curves of her flesh that caught me deep in my throat.

"This is yours, Nat. You bought it, even when it wasn't for sale. You're paying for it. Don't you want it anymore?"

She held her breasts in her hands, cupping them from below as if offering them for my approval.

"These belong to you now. You didn't get very much for your money, but they're yours." She spread her legs and stroked herself. "So is this. Aren't you going to use it?"

"Cut it out."

"Yes, sir, Mr. Crowley."

"Dammit—"

"Anything I can do to arouse you? Any new position you'd like to try? We can do it standing on our heads in a closet if you want, Mr. Crowley. Just say the word."

I slapped her. I hadn't meant to hit her that hard and she rubbed the side of her face.

"I'm sorry, Annie."

"Why? You've got the right."

"Annie…"

She turned from me. "I gather you don't want me in bed tonight. And that you're not too taken with my company. I'd like to get dressed and go downstairs and feed a slot machine."

"There's one here."

"I know. I'd like to get dressed and go downstairs and feed a slot machine. Is that all right with you?"

"Whatever you want," I said.

"And may I have fifty dollars to gamble with, Mr. Crowley?"

I gave her a hundred.

That was the third night. She went downstairs and I stayed where I was and drank myself to sleep. That was the third night, and it was a bad one.

Then there was the fourth night.

It started with her having too much to drink. She had been doing a lot of drinking since we got off the plane but the fourth night was heavier than usual. She was lapping up gin and tonic as though somebody were passing the Volstead Act all over again. We were downstairs in the casino and I was having a good run with the dice. I made a lot of passes—six, I think, which is a long string—and then sevened out on an easy point. I walked away from the table and took a drink away from her.

"Enough," I said.

"Never enough. You a cop?"

"No. Let's go upstairs, Annie."

"Want my drink."

I took her arm and she pouted at me. "Goddamned gangster. Steal a drink from a girl. You bum, Nat."

I got her into the elevator. She had a few more choice words on the way up but the kid who ran the elevator was used to it. He managed not to hear a thing. We left the elevator and I took her to our suite, opened a door and led her inside. "C'mon," I said. "You're going to bed." She shook my hand away and took a step backward. Her blue eyes were glassy now. Her lipstick was mostly gone.

"I just don't get it," she said.

"Don't get what?"

"There has to be a line somewhere. You get to a point where you know about things, you understand things, you have this— this awareness. Of what's going on. But then you wind up tolerating everything. You put up with things the squares couldn't stomach. You play around with crooks just to prove how hip you are. And you sleep with a rotten mindless killer—"

I slapped her, hard.

She stepped back. Her hand went to her face where I had hit her. The eyes were wide now and the glassy look was gone. She was sober, or close to it.

"You hit me again, Nat."

I didn't answer that one.

"I suppose I had it coming," she said. "I'm supposed to be part of the luggage, right? Something decorative. Something to carry around, something to leave in the bedroom. Not something to talk to or to be decent to. I didn't stay in my place, Nat, and I had it coming."

"Annie…"

Her next words came in a low whisper. "I'll make you sorry, Nat. I'm a person, goddamn it. I don't have to get stepped on."

I reached for her. Instead of catching her I caught her hand with my face. Something snapped.

"You damned—"

"I'm a whore, Nat. Nothing more, nothing less. You made me your whore and that's just what I am."

"Then strip!"

Her eyes flashed. "You want your money's worth?"

"I want my money's worth."

"Money for the airlines," she said. "Money for food and money for the hotel. Money to gamble away. Money for clothes and money for gin and gin and gin. I hope you get your money's worth, Nat."

She was wearing a black evening gown, simple and attractive. I watched her grip the gown at the top, in front, and rip. The dress was silk and it tore like children shrieking. It ripped all the way down. She stepped out of it and left it on the floor.

There was a bra, which went next. Then a pair of sheer panties. And then she stood in front of me quite naked and quite ridiculous in high-heeled black shoes.

She kicked off the shoes. She kicked hard and they sailed across the room, past me. One of them bounced off a wall. I looked at her again. She very deliberately drew the sheet and covers off the bed, then stretched out upon her back. Her eyes were still furious.

"Come on," she taunted. "You're paying for it."

I got my clothes off and went to her.

It was like that earlier time—all the anger, along with something that verged on hatred. I felt this wild need to possess, this strong urge to dominate. As for her, at first she played the cold machine, the automaton, the hired servant. Then something happened as I worked myself inside her. Something like war and again like murder. Not like love, not at all.

She made the small noises that an animal might make in a steel trap. She screamed once, and once she spoke my name—Crowley's name—with loathing.

But that doesn't mean she didn't respond physically in spite of herself. Her head rolled from side to side. Her body arched in such a way that she became a target I couldn't possibly miss. I became a sort of automatic revolver whose barrel kept sliding back and forth.

Her breathing was a rasp. Her thighs clenched. For me the sensation was something like being in a cushioned vise. Anne was hoarse and I was hoarse—from calling out gutter names to one another. And at last there was the explosion: the trigger pulled, the chambers emptied.

There were no words when it was over. I rolled away from her, exhausted, maybe a little afraid. My eyes closed by themselves. I listened to her ragged breathing. My back hurt, now, where she had scratched me with her nails. Before I had not even noticed the pain.

I thought I heard her crying quietly, sobbing. And then I didn't hear anything.

I slept soundly and completely. I hardly dreamed at all.

16

It was Wednesday, around eight in the evening. We'd had a pair of big lobsters at a seafood joint and now we were back at the High Rise. I sat on the edge of the bed listening to the water running in the john. Anne was taking another shower. She took them on the average of three times a day. A clean-living girl.

I picked up the telephone and gave Tony's number to the kid on the switchboard. I listened some more to Annie's shower while the switchboard put the call through. Then Tony's phone rang twice and he answered it

"Nat," I said. "How's the weather?"

"Rain. Nothing but rain, you lucky bastard."

"You're making me homesick."

"Having fun, Nat?"

"You could call it that. At least it isn't raining."

A pause. "Nothing wrong, is there?"

"Just that it's boring. Everybody shakes my hand and kisses my butt and points me toward the casino. They hurry to bring drinks to me. They step aside if I go near a crap table."

"That's because they love you."

"Yeah," I said. "I may be back tomorrow."

"Stay a week more," he said. "Have fun while you can. This city is a dog."

"At least it's our dog," I said.

Then there was some business talk. Nothing special—things were going smoothly. A troublesome detective had been shifted from Vice to Traffic Planning. Customs on the Peace Bridge had screwed up a minor heroin shipment. A fighter Tony liked was going for the light-heavy title and Tony had a few thou on him. I told him to get five hundred down for me, more to be sociable than anything else. That was that.

I put the phone back. The john door opened and Annie came out in a towel.

I said, "Get dressed."

"Where do we go now?"

I shrugged. "Downstairs. Where else?"

"Again?"

"Again."

"Oh, hell," she said. "Look, you go. I'll stay here and do some reading. Maybe I'll go to sleep, I'm a little tired."

"You slept all day, didn't you?"

"Uh-huh. But I'm so damned sick of the casino."

"It's not like we're there all the time. We took that ride last night."

"This whole stinking town is one big casino."

I told her she was right. I told her maybe we wouldn't stay in Vegas much longer, that the luxury and the leisure were beginning to get to me. And she told me, meekly enough to be subtly sarcastic, that I was the boss and we would do whatever I wanted. I said that what I wanted, for the time being, was for her to get dressed.

She got dressed.

The casino was beginning to fill up with idiots. Divorcees by the score were trying to nullify the laws of mathematics at the slot machines, dropping coins and yanking levers until they looked every bit as robotic as the machines that were taking their money. A collegiate type was explaining to an amateur whore why his system was sure-fire at the roulette wheel. A slender middle-aged man with a walrus mustache dealt blackjack and never smiled. I went to a teller's cage and traded money for chips. I halved the stack that the girl gave me, slipped one pile to Annie and kept the other deck for myself.

She liked to play single numbers, one chip to a roll. The odds were thirty-seven to one and the house paid off at the rate of thirty-five to one. I stuck to switching back and forth between red and black. The percentage was the same—it's always the same. That's why any roulette system is as stupid as any other— but it generally took me longer to lose my money.

For a girl who didn't want to play, Anne took enough of an interest in the game. I couldn't manage to get excited by the wheel.

It got tougher when I realized somebody was watching me.

He had one of those faces that disappear in a two-man crowd. His hair was sandy and his eyebrows were sandy and his complexion was sandy. He was five-seven or five-eight, not too thin and not too fat, with the blandest features ever. He had an ordinary nose and an ordinary chin and an ordinary mouth. He was probably forty, give or take five years, and undoubtedly married. He had that defeated look.

He was playing a slot machine and looking at me. I caught him at it once and he turned away. I went back to the roulette wheel but went on watching him out of the corner of my eye. Pretty soon he was looking at me again with a thoughtful expression on his unmemorable face.

The hell of it was, he looked familiar—in a very vague sort of a way. He hardly had a face you placed the minute you saw it. But I had seen him somewhere before.

And now he was watching me.

A tail? No, that was ridiculous. Nobody would be nuts enough to tail me in the middle of the High Rise's casino. Unless something was supposed to happen to me. Unless Tony had sent me to Vegas for a reason. To get hit, for example.

But why in hell would he do that? And why would it take so long?

I lit a cigarette and worried about these things. A waiter came by and I took a cold drink off his tray and worked on it. And then the sandy little man ended the confusion by coming over to me.

He said, "Uh—pardon me…"

I turned around and looked at him.

"I'm sorry as the devil," he said. "But there's something so familiar about you. I could swear we've met."

An Eastern accent. It fitted the clothes, which looked like New York.

"You must mean somebody else," I said.

"I don't think so. I rarely if ever forget a face. You weren't at Amherst, were you? I was class of thirty-nine."

"I never went there."

"Odd," he said. "I never forget a face."

He was more than a little stoned. He had a glass of something pale in one hand and periodically took a sip from it. Anne had turned from the roulette wheel and was helping me keep an eye on the little man. I finished my drink and gave the glass to a waiter.

"Perhaps the service," the little man said. "Navy?"

I shook my head. "I've done a little television work," I said. "Maybe you saw me on television."

He thought it over.

"It happens all the time," I went on. "You'd be surprised. People think I'm a long-lost friend just from seeing me on a television show."

"Maybe," he said. "Although—"

"That's what it must be."

"I'll remember," he said. "I'll remember, by God. I never forget a face."

He smiled, then apologized for having bothered me. He turned to walk away. He was carrying a pretty heavy load but he carried it neatly. He didn't stagger at all, didn't even wobble.

I left Anne at the roulette wheel. I crossed the floor, found a guard who knew me by sight. He gave me a large hello.

"The little guy," I said, nodding. "See him?"

"What about him?"

"That's what I want to know," I said. I folded a bill and passed it to him. "I want his name, who he is, where he's staying. Everything you can find out. Got it?"

"Sure," he said. "He some kind of a shill?"

"No."

"A chiseler? We get all kinds here. Want me to keep him out from now on, Mr. Crowley?"

"Just find out who he is," I said. "And let me know."

He said sure a few more times and went away. I wandered back to the roulette wheel. While I was gone black had come up three times straight, and nobody had bothered to push my chips off. I had a healthy stack riding. I let it ride.

"What was that all about, Nat?" Anne asked. She seemed just idly curious.

"Nothing," I said.

"An old friend?"

"A nobody. A bug."

"So why pay attention to him?"

Black came up. The croupier doubled my chips. I let them ride.

"No reason," I said. "To hell with him. You want another drink?"

"Not just yet."

I dug out fresh cigarettes. She took one and I used the lighter, the one Tony had given me. I looked from the lighter to the watch, the one Lou Baron had given me.

The wheel went around again. Red came up and the house raked in my chips.

We were in our room. It was later, a lot later, and I was just about ready to sack out for the night. There was a knock on the door, the discreet sort of knock that means the knocker is a hotel employee. I opened the door.

It was the guard. He said, "That guy, Mr. Crowley."

"Go on."

"His name is Albert Durkinsen. He's staying at the Marquis with his wife. He's in on a pleasure trip, pays with traveler's checks, tips a steady fifteen percent. He sounds as straight as a good cue."

"What's he do?"

"Buyer for a department store. I didn't get the name of the store."

I told him it didn't matter. And I asked the question to which I already knew the answer. I asked where this Albert Durkinsen lived with his wife and his department store.

"In Connecticut. In a town called—"

"Never mind," I interrupted, "I know the town."

Durkinsen never forgot a face. He must have seen mine twice a day in the papers and he never forgot a face. I wondered where he would be when he sobered up. He'd either place the face or not remember running into me at all. Maybe he would run around screaming about a wife-murderer at large in the peaceful state of Nevada. Maybe...

So we were on a plane leaving the following afternoon. We didn't run. I got up in the morning, yawned, stretched, yawned again, then rolled over and nudged Annie. 'This town stinks," I said. "I'm bored stiff."

So was she.

"Let's leave it," I said. "I'm sick of slot machines, I'm sick of roulette wheels, I'm sick of tourists. I'm even sick of hotels where they fall on their faces to serve you. It's a pain in the neck."

"Breakfast first," she said. "Then we'll pack."

We had scotch and eggs for breakfast, which isn't as bad as it sounds. Then we packed. I called the desk and told them to reserve the nearest jet to Buffalo. I called Dan Gordon, went downstairs to see him and told him I had to run and that he ran the best damned hotel in the world. He laughed like a baboon, pounded my arm, and told me to give Tony his love. I told him I'd kiss Tony for him. Gordon had an even bigger laugh over that one. When we got downstairs I signed my tab. They had a Caddy waiting for us and we made our plane with time to spare.

The flight back was a fast one, a good one. We took a cab in from the airport. I told Annie to pick up her stuff from her old apartment in the morning and let the cabby take us both to the Stennett.

"You live here," I said "With me."

"That's the rule?"

"Your landlord threw you out," I said. "You might as well take advantage of my hospitality."

She didn't argue. From the Stennett I called Tony. He sounded glad to hear from me.

"I'll be damned," he said. "You really couldn't stay away."

I said, "It was fun. But I figured you'd go nuts without me."

17

October was a lazy month. The days got a little shorter. The trees dropped their leaves and the police dropped the lid on a few of our numbers locations on William Street. That was the closest October got to being hectic. We got word of the raid just four hours ahead of time and we had to work fast. The boys minding the stores scouted around for some neighborhood loafers who could use a hundred fast dollars for thirty days' work. Then our boys went home and the loafers waited for the cops behind the counters. The police came on schedule and arrested the patsies —and the next day we had business as usual. The newspapers were happy, the townsfolk were assured they had a functioning police force and nobody got hurt.

That was October. I spent it at my office, at Cassino's, at Noomie's, at the Stennett. There was a week, maybe two weeks, when I sat on the edge of my chair and waited for Albert Durkinsen to remember where he had seen my pretty face. Evidently he forgot all about me. Or, if he remembered, he decided to let it lie. Or, if he went screaming to the nearest cop, the cop wrote off little Albert as a screwball to be neatly ignored. Whatever way the incident played itself out, Albert from Connecticut was a man to be forgotten and Donald Barshter was deader than a dozen doornails.

My job was easy and got to be surprisingly satisfying. The job involved business and at the same time it was illegal—and the combination got to be a hell of an interesting one. I had the inside track and the inside story, which kept the job exciting.

But when I was in my office with my door closed and my secretary buffing her nails and a pile of papers and correspondence on my desk in front of me, I was just another straight-and-narrow businessman all over again. It was bookkeeping and figure-juggling and memo-writing, and only the pay and the underworld undertone made the job different from being somebody's accountant. Or from selling insurance. But that was enough for me. I'd always been good at the work, and this way it didn't bore me.

And I was starting to like Buffalo. It was my town now—this made a difference. The trip to Las Vegas—Tony's idea, not mine—had been a good move. It made coming back to Buffalo a pleasure.

So that was October and it was pleasant. I had a closet filled with suits and a bank account filled with money. There was a safe-deposit box, also filled with money, and on that money I didn't have to pay taxes. There was Berman's basement, where we still played poker once a week, and there were half a dozen nightclubs where they always had a table free for me. There was the place at the Stennett which got more and more like a home.

And when I wanted her, there was Anne Bishop.

She wasn't the same girl, not exactly. A mistress is not the same thing as a girlfriend. Anne was a mistress now and her independence was over and done with. She lived with me and slept with me. I gave her money for clothes, money for books, money for her to do as she pleased with. We still had our cute conversations but they were milder now, never so fierce as they had grown before. We still had our probing sessions, Anne playing her "Who Is This Nathaniel Crowley?" game, but they were fewer, farther between and infinitely subtler. We still had our kicks but they were somehow a different sort, our roles more clearly defined. I hadn't had reason to slap her again, since Vegas. She hadn't wielded any shivs.

"You ought to break down," she said one night. "You ought to make an honest woman out of me, Nat."

"That a proposal?"

"Just an idea. Why don't we get married?"

"Sure," I said. "Maybe we could find one of those split-levels. I hear you can get a thirty-year mortgage with no sweat these days."

"Not a split-level. A huge stone house with a lot of land around it and respectable neighbors. Gangsters love to brag about their respectable neighbors. I watched *The Untouchables* and I know all about gangsters."

"I know the program. It's about lower-caste Hindus. In India."

"That's the one," she said.

"Are you untouchable?" I asked.

"Not exactly. Why?"

I said, "Come here and I'll show you."

And I showed her. We'd grown used to our roles, and it was not murderous now. There was no fight to have the upper hand. You could almost think of it as making love—if you squinted. If you forgot about how we got here, about the things we'd said and done. The things I'd said, the things I'd done.

She played the let's-get-married record again a few days later. This time there were violins in the background. She almost made marriage sound interesting but I remembered Ellen too well to really meditate about it. Besides, for obvious reasons, marriage was impossible.

"I'm twice shy," I said.

"Meaning you were once bitten?"

"Something like that."

"That's interesting," she said thoughtfully. "Tell me all your troubles, Nat Crowley. Tell me about your past love and your past life. Do you have an exciting past?"

"No past at all."

"Where were you born?"

"I wasn't," I told her. "I sprang full-blown from the brow of Johnny Torrio. Don't you read your crime comics? They're part of American mythology."

"What happened to her?"

I looked at her. "To who? You lost me."

"To your wife."

"Oh," I said. "She left me. She ran away with a pencil sharpener. It was very sad."

"I guess you don't want to talk about it, do you?"

"Oh, I don't mind," I said. "But I've got this terrible allergy—I break out whenever I'm near a sharp pencil."

Then October disappeared and it was November. It was a Sunday night, late, but neither Annie nor I felt like sleeping. We got the doorman to find the Lincoln for us and climbed into it. The first snow of the season was falling on us. It was scattered, skitterish snow, melting as it hit the pavement, but it was enough for me to keep the Lincoln's top up.

I headed the car east and parked down the block from Noomie's. It was as bad a neighborhood as ever and nobody with sense parked a decent car there. But the kids in the neighborhood knew whose car the Lincoln was. Nobody would hotwire it or break off the radio aerial or otherwise foul things up. We got out and walked through the falling snow to the doorway. The coffee-colored hostess passed us through with a smile. We found a table in front and ordered drinks.

Pete Moscato was there with a blonde I'd seen around

before. Pete was Angie's younger brother, a pretty sharp kid moving up fast. I think he admired me or something. Pete and his blonde came over and sat down at our table. We listened to the combo on stage go through a hard jazz arrangement of "Night in Tunisia." Then the combo switched to a slow Cole Porter thing and the four of us got up to dance. After one number the combo worked on another slow one and we traded girls. Annie danced with Pete and I moved his blonde around the floor. It turned into a sort of vertical rape—either she was madly in love with me or she wanted to aid Pete's progress in local crookdom, or that was the only way she knew to dance. Whatever, her hot little hips kept bouncing at me and her body wrapped itself around me like a second skin. By the time we got off the floor I needed the fresh drink that was waiting for me.

We talked some more. Then Pete remembered something he had to do and took his blonde bombshell away.

Annie raised her glass to me. "Have a nice time?"

"Wonderful."

"I'm jealous as hell," she said. "Nat, can I go to New York?"

"Huh?"

"I want to go on a buying spree," she said. "I want to leave your money all over Fifth Avenue."

"What prompted this?"

"I read an article on what the well-dressed whore is wearing this year. I'm out of style. Can I fly down for a few days?"

"I'll get lonely."

"Why should you? There are loads of blondes in this town. Hair color so natural only their druggist knows for sure."

I lit cigarettes for us. She drew hard on hers and blew a little smoke across the table at me.

"New York," she said. "Okay?"

"Sure," I said.

"I'll need money."

"How much?"

"I don't know," she said. "A few hundred. Enough for plane fare and a room and meals and to buy clothes with. Not too much."

"You learn fast, don't you?"

"I've got the name," she said. "I might as well have the fun."

The next day I wrote her an impressive check and she scurried off to the bank to cash it. That night she called the airport and made her reservation. The following afternoon I drove her to the airport. It was ugly weather. A little snow had managed to pile up on the sidewalks and now a frigid rain was melting the snow and putting a raw edge to the air. The clouds were black. Annie was worried that her flight might be canceled but I told her they flew in everything nowadays, especially on shortie trips like the one she was taking. I dropped her at the terminal entrance while I found a place to park in the big open lot. She had one piece of light gray luggage. I parked the car and carried her bag inside.

She bought her ticket and checked her baggage. I followed her over to the newsstand where she picked out a few books to shorten the trip. Then we grabbed coffee and waited for her flight to be called.

When that happened I walked most of the way to the plane with her. Moments of parting are funny ones. I held her hand a little more tightly than usual. When she put her face up to be kissed I wanted to hold her very close, to say something sweet to her, something nice.

But I didn't know how.

So I handed her a lopsided smile and chucked her under the chin. "Be good," I told her. "Don't stay away too long."

"I won't."

"Here," I said. I slipped her an extra bill, a big one. She palmed it and smiled ambiguously. Then she turned and walked away from me to the plane.

Anne was gone a week. It was a long week. She left on a Tuesday, in the afternoon, and she came back on a Monday, at night, and the days in the middle were curiously empty ones. It was a week when I would have gladly buried myself in work but there just wasn't that much work to do. I spent all of Wednesday and most of Thursday at the free-form desk in my office writing meaningless numbers on sheets of memo paper, doodling mechanically and waiting for time to pass. It passed, but slowly.

Wednesday night I got moodily drunk at a quiet little bar not far from the Stennett. Finally I went home and slept.

Thursday night there was the poker game at Berman's. Tony picked me up and ran me over. I held good cards and played them well and won around a hundred dollars. Our game went for higher stakes lately—all the players were Tony's boys from a while back and all of them had been living better since Baron had left the scene. When dawn broke the game broke, too. I put my winnings in my wallet and let Tony run me home.

We stopped on the way for ham and eggs. Tony put down a cup of coffee and looked at me. "I got some advice," he said. "But you don't have to listen to it."

"I always listen to your advice."

"This is different. Personal advice. The kind you can ignore."

"Go on."

He drank more coffee. "When your woman comes back," he said, "marry her."

I took out a cigarette and tapped it on the smooth tabletop. I lighted it and looked at Tony.

"It's not my business," he said.

I blew out smoke.

"Just an idea," he said. "You don't play around, Nat. You've got a steady deal with one broad. A good girl, not just a walking, talking piece. I knew her a long time ago. She's a good kid."

"So?"

"So it's not just a shack-up. Right?"

I didn't answer. I drank my coffee. It wasn't bad coffee. I signaled the waitress to bring me another cup.

"I'm not saying this right," he said. "I talk fine when it's business. This is different. So all I do is stick my foot down my throat. Want me to shut up, Nat?"

"You're doing fine."

Tony shrugged. "I don't know," he said. "Look, there are different kinds of racket people. Some like a good time and high living. Nothing tying them down. Maybe I'm like that. Others are like Berman. A house, a wife, kids and to hell with the excitement. Maybe you're like that. I don't mean a house in the suburbs, a country-club scene, any of that. You know what I mean?"

I nodded.

"You went nuts in Vegas," he said. "Gambling isn't your kick, chasing isn't your kick, nightlife isn't your kick. You can do those things, but they don't send you to the moon. Hell, I'm preaching a sermon. Let's let it lie."

"Fine."

"But it's something to think about, Nat."

"Sure," I said. "It's something to think about."

I tipped the waitress and picked up our checks. Then we left the place and he drove me home.

It was a dull and thoughtful weekend. I did more drinking than usual but never quite managed to go over the edge. I drank and stayed strangely sober.

I thought about Tony Quince and his diagnosis and prescription. So Nat Crowley was nothing but a family man at heart. I tossed that one around and remembered another family man who used to sell insurance. Maybe he hadn't changed so damned much after all. Maybe few things change.

On Sunday night it was hard to sleep. People paraded through my mind, many people, all dead now. Ellen led the parade, of course, and too many people followed on her heels. There was Jack Garstein, a family man from Philadelphia. There was Scarpino and Johnny Carr and Leon Spiro and a tough little blonde with a slit throat. There was *To Nat From Lou Baron* and there was Porky, who hadn't talked much. My private Hit Parade, which may or may not be a bad pun.

I got a wire Monday morning telling me what plane to meet. It was snowing out, big flakes that piled up in drifts. I ate breakfast and drove around in the Lincoln. I took a ride through the cemetery and managed to find Scarpino's grave. I remembered him kissing his father and going for a final ride, the inevitable final ride. I remembered Scarpino's face when he saw the grave, an open wound in the earth. And the dirt falling on him, and Tony and Angie and I walking silently back to the car.

Anne's plane was supposed to land at nine. I was at the airport by eight-thirty. I had coffee and rolls in the airport coffee shop. Then I leafed through an early newspaper while I waited for the plane. It had stopped snowing sometime in the late afternoon and her plane was supposed to arrive on time. It did.

I tried to decide whether I felt like a man waiting for a mistress or a husband waiting for a wife. It was hard to say.

Anne came off the plane looking lovely. She'd had her hair done in New York and it was neat and pretty. She came to me with steady eyes and her skin rosy from the cold air. I kissed cool lips.

"I missed you," I said.

"You did?"

And somehow I had run out of words. I took her hand and we walked over to the baggage counter to wait for her gray suitcase. We talked aimlessly. She told me New York had been fine, the weather had been good there. I asked her if she had bought many clothes. She said there hadn't been much she had bought but that she had seen a few good shows and had gone to some nice restaurants. There had been a good cool jazz group at the Blind Spot, and she'd been there once or twice.

Her suitcase came. She traded a baggage check for it and I carried it. It wasn't heavy. We walked to the door.

"Wait here," I said. "I'll bring the car around."

"I can come with you."

"The snow's deep. Wait here."

I brought the Lincoln over. I put her suitcase in the back. Anne got beside me in front. The conversation on the way to the Stennett was small talk. I asked her if she wanted to stop for a bite. She said she had had dinner on the plane and wasn't hungry right now. I gave the Lincoln to the doorman and we went into the lobby and rode the elevator upstairs. I opened the door to the apartment and followed her inside. She made drinks while I hung up our coats.

We touched glasses and I sipped my drink. She was still drinking gin and tonic, even with snow on the ground.

"Annie…"

"Don't call me Annie," she said.

"Why not?"

"Not anymore," she said. "That's over now."

Her voice was very odd. I was missing something and I wasn't sure what it was. I offered her a cigarette. She shook her head. I took one for myself and lighted it with my *To Nat From Tony* lighter.

"Okay," I said. "I'll bite. What do I call you?"

"Miss Bishop."

"Isn't that kind of formal?"

"You call me Miss Bishop," she said. "And I'll call you Mr. Barshter."

18

"It was only a matter of time," she said. "I knew there was something to look for, some kind of secret. You certainly weren't Nat Crowley. There were too many things out of line, too many inconsistencies. It was just a question of knowing what to look for and where to look."

Black hair, all neat, every strand in place. Blue eyes. Now a very icy blue.

"You were never Nat Crowley from Miami. And you weren't a racket type, not from the start. You were feeling your way. And gradually you grew into yourself, didn't you? It was something to watch. You got harder and tougher until you turned into Nat Crowley. And by then I didn't even like you anymore, Nat. I mean Don, don't I? Is that what they called you? Don?"

"I don't remember. It's been a long time."

She was smiling. "Then I'll stick to Mr. Barshter. It's easier, I suppose. It keeps everything on a businesslike plane."

"How did you find out?"

She ignored the question. "I wasn't even trying at first. I told you not to tell me too much. Do you remember? I knew there was something to look for and I didn't want to find it. I thought we could have something nice. I thought you could live your life and I could live my life and the two of us could build a nice scene between us. Something easy. Something that let me be me."

I put down my drink without finishing it. I put out my cigarette in an ashtray.

"You wouldn't let it stay that way, Nat. You see what I mean? I can't help calling you Nat—you grew into yourself that completely. And you had to make me fit the new pattern. You had to

get the right hold on me. You never should have made me come
to Vegas with you. That was a big mistake. It made me hate you."

I didn't say anything. She was talking calmly, levelly. Her
eyes had gone an even icier shade of blue, or maybe it was my
imagination.

"From there on I was looking. I noticed that drunk both-
ering you in the casino at the High Rise. I noticed how you sent
a guard chasing after him. I was awake when he came back to
report like a good little soldier. I heard the drunk's name and
address."

"And it was my home town."

"It was your home town," she said. "We left Vegas the next
day and I knew this Albert Durkinsen was something out of the
past, something before Nat Crowley. I let it go for a while. I
tried to figure out a little more—maybe I waited for you to turn
back into a human being again. I don't know. Then I flew to
New York."

"And went to my home town?"

"Eventually. Not at first—first I went through back issues of
the *New York Times* looking for Durkinsen, which didn't do
anything for me. Then I tried Nathaniel Crowley and drew the
same blank. But I didn't expect to get anything that way. I took
a train for your Connecticut town and went through the back
issues of the newspaper there. I started two weeks after I met you
in Buffalo and worked my way back. It wasn't hard to find you,
Nat. You were all over the front pages. You're a local celebrity.
You murdered your wife and stuffed her in a closet. That's big
news."

I looked down at my hands. My fingers weren't even shaking.
I was calmer than I thought possible.

"Then I went back to New York. I found a lawyer, a very respectable lawyer. I left a letter with him. Know what it said?"

"I can guess."

"I'll save you the trouble. I'm supposed to call him once a day. When I don't, he mails out a few copies of that letter. One goes to the police, in Buffalo. Another goes to your home town police. A third goes to the FBI. That's my own personal insurance policy, Nat. But you know all about insurance, don't you?"

I didn't answer her.

"That leaves you sitting on a hot seat," she continued. "You can get nailed even if you don't kill me. All I have to do is get killed by a car on my way across the street. I can catch pneumonia and die of it and when I don't call that lawyer—then off go my letters. If anything happens to me, Nat, the roof falls in on you."

I lighted another cigarette. "What's the pitch? Blackmail?"

"Extortion."

"There's a difference?"

"It's only blackmail if I send you a threatening letter. It's a technical difference, that's all. Extortion carries a lighter sentence." The smile was back again. "And a much lighter sentence than murder."

"What do they do to murderers in Connecticut?"

"Don't you know?"

"I never bothered to find out."

"They electrocute them," she said. "They strap them in a chair and throw a switch. But you don't have to sit in that kind of chair, Nat. Not so long as I live."

"What's in the letter?"

"It's a short letter. Just who you are and what you did and where you are now. Plus a few other names of people you killed here in Buffalo. But that's extra. You could get away with those killings, Nat. But you couldn't get out from under murdering your wife. Not with all the connections in the world."

And that was funny, because Ellen's death had been man-slaughter. The others were first-degree murder, and those I could get away with—if only on the grounds that New York no longer gives the death sentence except for cop killings.

I asked her what the deal was.

"First of all," she said, "I move out. Out of here and into some other hotel. Maybe I'll start with the Malmsly. Is it nice there?"

"It's all right."

"I'll be Miss Anne Bishop again. Not somebody's mistress. Just a nice independent girl. I'll move out and tomorrow you can come to see me. Bring money, Nat. Ten thousand dollars."

"That's a lot of money."

"You can spare it. I want it in cash, of course."

"And it's only the beginning."

She shrugged easily. "Probably. Ten thousand dollars would last me a long time. But I've got the upper hand, Nat. I've got a hold. When you have a hold, then you have to put on the pressure. That's why I went to Las Vegas with you. That's why you're going to pay me a lot of money for a long time. I've got you by the throat. I don't intend to let go."

"You used to be a pretty nice kid," I said.

"You changed me."

"Nobody changes," I said. "The more things change, the more they remain the same. I guess it holds for people, too."

"What do you mean?"

"It doesn't matter. Do you hate me that much?"

"It's not hate. It was never love and it never got to be hate, not exactly. Do you know what I mean?"

"Probably."

She walked to the closet and got her coat. I didn't try to stop her, nor did I help her on with the coat. I just stood and watched her get into it.

"Ten thousand dollars in cash," she said. "I'll be expecting you tomorrow. Make it around three in the afternoon. My lawyer will be waiting for a call at four-thirty. I don't want to disappoint him. If I did, he'd put some letters in the mail."

"And that would be unpleasant."

"Wouldn't it?" She smiled very sweetly. "Tomorrow at three. Pleasant dreams, Nat."

I dreamed no dreams, pleasant or otherwise. I did not sleep that night. After she had gone I started to build myself a drink, then changed my mind and emptied the rye and soda in the sink. Instead I lit another cigarette and started pacing the floor. I did this until the sun came up and I didn't get the least bit tired. When I stopped, the ashtray was overflowing for the fourth time and I was beginning to wear out the carpet.

I had breakfast at the diner around the corner. I didn't feel like eating but I forced a plate of scrambled eggs down my throat and washed my mouth out with coffee. I smoked another cigarette. I went back to my apartment, showered, shaved and put on a fresh suit.

When your woman comes back, marry her, Tony had said.

Thanks, Tony. I could do with a little advice.

You don't play around, Nat. You've got a steady deal with one broad. A good girl, not just a walking, talking piece. I knew her a long time ago. She's a good kid.

She was, then.

You went nuts in Vegas. Gambling isn't your kick, chasing isn't your kick, nightlife isn't your kick. You can do those things, but they don't send you to the moon. Hell, I'm preaching a sermon. Let's let it lie.

Let's.

19

I left the Stennett again around nine. I stopped at an army surplus store and bought a money belt. The clerk didn't know what I was talking about at first. Then he found one somewhere in the back and sold it to me. I left it in the bag he put it in and carried it downtown to the bank.

I went downstairs to the safe-deposit vault. A thin gray man led me inside, then used first his key and then my key on the box I'd rented, took it from its niche in the wall and gave it to me. I carried it across to one of the private booths along the wall and locked myself up with it. I opened the box and took out my money.

There was a lot of it, all tax-free, all mine. I counted out seven thousand dollars. There was a lot more upstairs in the checking account, enough so that I could pay Annie with no trouble at all.

I filled the belt with money. I hung my coat and jacket over the back of the chair, opened my pants and fitted the belt around me, underneath my slacks. I got dressed again, carried the empty box outside and gave it to the thin gray man. He used his key and my key to lock the box back in place.

I went to the nearest five-and-dime store. I bought a cloth airlines bag, a package of absorbent cotton and a bottle of black hair dye. I walked farther downtown, turned east and went to three secondhand clothing stores. In one of them I bought a pair of work shoes in fairly good shape. In another I bought a pair of denim slacks and a plain flannel shirt. In the third I picked up a secondhand lumber jacket, a little frayed around the collar but in pretty good condition otherwise. I loaded the airlines bag with everything but the jacket and took a cab to the bus terminal. I found a locker and stowed the bag and the jacket in it.

Around noon I had lunch downtown. I ate a few hamburgers and drank a few cups of coffee. I still wasn't at all tired. Then I walked around downtown Buffalo. The weather was clear, a little snow underfoot but none falling—the town looked better than usual. I passed my office building and then went back and rode up to my office on the eighteenth floor. My secretary wasn't around. I opened a few letters and left them on the desk. I looked around to see if there were anything I wanted. There wasn't.

From the window I could see most of the city. I stood by it for a few minutes and watched cars crawl through the streets like fat shiny beetles. I thought about the town. It had been good to me.

I used my office phone to call the air terminal. I reserved a seat on a plane to Philadelphia leaving Buffalo at a few minutes to four. I used the name Nathaniel Crowley. I hung up and left the office.

The air was cooler now. I walked around for a few minutes. I looked at my watch. It was after two.

I didn't go right away. I walked around a little more, thinking it over, trying to decide. It wasn't absolutely necessary, wasn't necessary at all. In fact it meant taking another chance, an extra chance. But it was something I had to do.

Maybe it was an idea of justice that had seeped into Nat Crowley. A notion of balance, and right and wrong. Maybe it was a poetic hangover from the Donald Barshter period. There was poetry in it, certainly. And I was still both people, a hard-to-figure combination of Barshter and Crowley.

Whatever it was, it had to be that way.

So at two-thirty I walked into the Malmsly. I gave my name at the desk and they called her on the phone. She said to send me straight up. I went straight up.

Her room was on a high floor. I knocked at the door and she opened it for me. She was wearing a white cashmere sweater and a pair of black toreador pants. I looked at them.

"New York," she said. "I bought them on my shopping trip. How do I look, Don?"

"You look fine. We're back to Don again?"

"For the time being. Do you like the name?"

"I don't mind it."

"Good." She turned her back on me and walked to the window. She looked out, leaning against the sill. She turned around slowly, her eyes amused.

"Did you bring the money, Don?"

"Sure."

"That's good. It costs a lot of money to phone a lawyer in New York every day. This ten thousand will ease the burden."

"I'm sure it will."

"It will. May I have it now, Don?"

There was a bottle of gin on the bureau. It was about half full. That was sort of an added touch, although it would have been even better if it had been a scotch bottle. You can't have everything.

"The money, Don."

I took out my wallet and tossed it past her, onto the bed. She looked at me, then at the wallet. And she turned around to pick it up.

"This isn't ten thousand," she said. "Are you out of your—"

I hit her before she finished the sentence. I picked up the gin bottle and in one motion brought it down on her head. The cork was in the bottle. Not a drop spilled.

One blow wasn't enough. She went down, sprawling at the foot of the bed, and she was too dazed and groggy to scream. I hit her again and again and I went right on beating her over the head until her skull was soft and it was very definitely over. I took her pulse, which was only a matter of form. She was very dead.

I looked at her again. That was a mistake, because what I saw was that fine black hair and those fine blue eyes—blind eyes now. And I saw also, for just an instant or so, an image of what could have been. In another world, perhaps. Long ago, in another country. The wench was dead now. I had murdered her.

I put the gin bottle down. I took my wallet and returned it to my jacket pocket. I did not wipe fingerprints from anything. That would have been silly.

The hallway was quiet. I stepped out of it, closing the door and locking it. I rang for the elevator. It came along soon enough and I rode to the lobby and walked out into the street.

I took a taxi to the airport. On the way I made small talk with the driver. He let me off at the entrance to the terminal. I went inside, walked over to one of the flight desks and picked up the ticket I'd reserved earlier. I paid for it with a crisp, fresh hundred-dollar bill.

Then I wandered outside again and caught another cab. I had him drop me at the bus terminal. There I got my lumber jacket and airlines bag from the locker I'd stuffed it in. I carried them upstairs to the men's room. There was a large booth at one end where for a quarter you could do anything from taking a bath to sleeping for a quick hour. It was one of several favorite places for junkies looking for a spot to shoot up. I dropped my quarter in the slot and went inside.

I took off my coat, my jacket, my pants, my shoes. I washed

up, then uncapped the bottle of hair dye and rubbed it into my hair. I worked on it until my hair was black instead of mud-colored. Then I put the bottle of dye on the edge of the sink and played around with the absorbent cotton. I packed cotton in my cheeks, under my upper lip, I checked myself in the mirror. It made a difference. How much of a difference was something I couldn't tell for sure.

I dressed again. I put on the plaid flannel shirt, the denim work pants. I unlaced the work shoes and got my feet into them. I tied them. They weren't as comfortable as my thirty-dollar pair but I had no complaint. The work shoes had not cost thirty dollars.

I put my own clothes back in the airlines bag. I took all my cards from my wallet, shredded them and flushed them down the toilet. I folded the money and slipped it into a pocket of the work pants. I dropped the wallet into the airlines bag. It was a shame to part with it, but men in denim pants don't carry alligator wallets.

I looked at my watch—*To Nat From Lou Baron.* I dropped it into the bag. I looked at my lighter—*To Nat From Tony*—and dropped it into the bag too.

I checked myself in the mirror again. Not perfect, not close to perfect, but as good as I was going to be able to do. I got into the lumber jacket, zipped the airlines bag, dropped my own coat over my arm, picked up the bag and left the men's room. I walked down a flight of stairs and went back to the lockers. I found one, used a dime on it and left the bag and the coat there. They would open that locker in time, but not for a few days.

Fifteen minutes later a bus left Buffalo headed for Cincinnati with a half-dozen minor stops along the way. I was on it.

❖

We hit Cleveland at nine, then headed south and west. I sat in my seat and smoked a cigarette. An old man with whiskey breath dozed next to me. I tried to relax. It didn't work.

The lawyer would have mailed the letters by now. Tomorrow the FBI would get a letter, the Buffalo police would get a letter, the home town police would get a letter. By that time, or even by now, somebody would have found Annie's body at the foot of her bed in her room at the Malmsly.

I put out my cigarette. A minute later I scratched a match and set another one on fire. The bus kept rolling along an empty highway. I had a ticket to Cinci but somewhere along the way I was getting off. I had no idea where.

The big towns were out now. Big towns were mob towns and mob people would be looking for me. I knew too much to go on outside the organization. The mob wouldn't look too hard but people would be keeping eyes open.

That left small towns. And a stranger stuck out like an infected pinkie in a small town.

Last time it had been easier. Last time only a few people had been looking for me and last time I'd been able to run with my own face and my own hair. Now it wasn't safe to do that any longer. Now I had black hair and cotton in my cheeks. Someday somebody would notice this. Somebody would wonder why, and then…

I finished my cigarette and lit another one. My throat was raw from a few thousand cigarettes. I was tired but sleep was impossible. I didn't even try.

Big towns, small towns. I had seven thousand dollars around my waist and no place to run to. Barshter was dead and Crowley was dead and I didn't even have a new name picked out. Or a new personality, or a new person, or anything. I wondered who I would be, how I could hope to bring it off.

I sat in darkness and smoked. The drunk next to me started snoring. I went on smoking.

The Connecticut authorities were looking for Donald Barshter. The New York authorities were looking for Nat Crowley. The FBI was looking for us both.

I wondered who they'd catch first.

NAT CROWLEY, WE HARDLY KNEW YE
An Afterword by Lawrence Block

It was sometime in the summer of 2010, five years ago as I write these lines, that Miriam Parker, Mulholland Books' resident Marketing Genius, recalled a story she'd heard about a lost early book of mine. Was I still searching for it? And would I like to enlist the help of a multitude of readers by recounting the saga on Mulholland's new blog?

Well, why not? A post on their site could only help *A Drop of the Hard Stuff*, the Matthew Scudder novel Mulholland was about to publish. And who was to say that someone, while reading the blog, might not have a lightbulb take shape directly above his or her head? "Crikey," Gentle Reader might say aloud. "I remember that book! Why, I even have a copy, shelved between *Forever Amber* and *A Boy's Life of Gilles de Rais*. Here's my chance to help a favorite author and enhance the world of literature."

Hey, it could happen.

So I wrote the following piece, which appeared in short order on the Mulholland website:

HEY SINNER MAN, WHERE'D YOU GO?
by Lawrence Block

You've probably heard the song. It's a spiritual, and it starts out something like this:

> *Hey sinner man, where you gonna run to?*
> *Hey sinner man, where you gonna run to?*
> *Hey sinner man, where you gonna run to?*
> *All on that day…*

In the verses that follow, we learn that ol' Sinner Man has run to the north, the east, the south, and the west, to the rock and to the hill and to any number of other sites, and nowhere can he find a place to hide from divine judgment. Then he runs to the Lord, and that turns out to be the answer.

When you look at it like that, it sounds pretty lame, doesn't it? I'm reminded of the truly awful actor in the truly dreadful showcase production of *Hamlet*. When some audience members walk out during the famous soliloquy, he breaks character and cries out, "Hey, don't blame me—I'm not the one who wrote this shit!"

What I did write, however, was a crime novel I called *Sinner Man*. It was my first crime novel, though it was a long way from being my first published novel. (And it was also a long way from being my first published crime novel, as you'll see.)

If memory serves (and I might point out that, if memory truly served, there'd be no need for me to write this piece, or you to read it) I wrote *Sinner Man* sometime in the winter of 1959-60. In the summer of 1957, after two years at Antioch College, I'd dropped out to take a job as an editor at Scott Meredith Literary Agency. I was there for a year, and wrote and sold a dozen or so stories of my own during that time. Then I dropped in again, or tried to; I went back to Antioch, but by then I was writing books for Harry Shorten at Midwood and had sold a lesbian novel to Fawcett Crest, and I had more books and stories to write, and what the hell did I care about *Paradise Lost* or *Humphrey Clinker*, let alone *The Development of Physical Ideas*? So at the end of the year I went to New York and took a room at the Hotel Rio, where I wrote another book for Midwood and, as my first for Bill Hamling's Nightstand Books, one I called *Campus Tramp*.

And then I dropped out again, but this time it was the school's idea. "We think you would be happier elsewhere," said the note from Student Personnel Committee, and who was I to say them nay? They got that one right, and I moved back to my parents' house in Buffalo and went on writing.

And among the books I wrote, unlike my standing-order assignments for Midwood and Nightstand, was one I called *Sinner Man*.

Now the books I'd been writing were erotica, but the short stories I'd been writing and selling to magazines like *Manhunt* and *Trapped* and *Guilty* were crime fiction, and I'd had it in mind all along to move up to crime novels. (And then, of course, in the fullness of time I would move up to the pinnacle of mainstream literary fiction, and all the girls who'd rejected me would want to kill themselves. Yeah, right.)

So I started writing about a thirty-something guy, in advertising or something corporate, married and living in Danbury, Connecticut. (I'm pretty sure it was Danbury. But I suppose it could have been Darien, or even Hartford. Definitely Connecticut, though.) And one evening, possibly in the wake of an extra pre-prandial martini, he shoves his wife and she falls down and hits her head and, just like that, she's dead.

Hey, these things happen.

So he reaches for the phone to call the police, and thinks maybe he should call his lawyer first, and decides that, rather than call *anyone*, what he really wants to do is Get Out of Dodge. (Except I think it was Danbury.)

He gets on a train and gets off in Buffalo. (That seemed logical to me. Half the time I got on a train, I wound up getting off in Buffalo. The other half the time I got *on* in Buffalo and got off somewhere else. Never Danbury, however. As best I recall.)

And in Buffalo he's faced with a problem. Like, how is he going to make a living, given that he's wanted in Connecticut for uxoricide? His fingerprints aren't on file, but they've got his name and photos of him, so he can't walk into National Gypsum or Bethlehem Steel, plop down his Social Security card and his driver's license, and apply for an executive position. What can he do that will enable him to live life off the grid? (That wasn't an expression yet, *off the grid*, but that's where he had to live.)

Well, how about organized crime? Gangsters wouldn't ask to see ID. And if he acted like a gangster, and hung out where the gangsters hung out, well, he might get killed if he rubbed someone the wrong way, but they weren't gonna turn him in to the cops, were they?

So that's what he did. And then the story just went on from there, though I can't claim to remember what happened. I don't know what his original name was, or what new name he took for himself. I think there was a card game in the house of a guy named Berman. I think our hero fit in nicely with the gang, and had a knack for criminality, and then there was a faction fight in the gang. Or something.

See, I really don't remember a whole lot about the book. Danbury, Buffalo, gangsters, and Berman. And I'm not 100% sure about Berman.

✲

I finished the book, and I sent it to Henry Morrison, who was my agent at Scott Meredith. He sent it around, and around it went, garnering the same sort of rejections everywhere. No end of editors said they liked the way I wrote, and would be glad for a look at my next book. That was fine, but what I was hoping for was that one of them would want to buy *this* book, as it was the one I had for sale. But the consensus seemed to be that, while the writing was commendable, the book as a whole was not—and it went on making the rounds.

Meanwhile, I got married and moved back to New York, setting up housekeeping first on West 69th Street and then farther uptown on Central Park West. My father died, my daughter Amy was born, and in the spring of 1962 my wife and daughter and I moved back to Buffalo where we bought a house.

(The house was actually in a suburb called Tonawanda. In Thomas Perry's dazzling series, his heroine Jane Whitefield lives in Tonawanda. So it's possible to write good crime fiction set in Western New York, even if I couldn't seem to do it.)

By now I'd sold two crime novels, *Grifter's Game* and *Coward's Kiss*, to Fawcett Gold Medal. (They called the first one *Mona* and the second one *Death Pulls a Doublecross*. Hey, don't get me started, okay?) And shortly after we'd settled into our house in Tonawanda, Henry sent *Sinner Man* to Random House, where Lee Wright was publishing my good friend Donald E. Westlake. Lee read the book and saw something there, and I got on a train (yeah, I did that a lot) and went to New York to discuss it with her.

Ah, if only life had an Undo button. I went to Lee's office and had this weird conversation with her, during which she suggested various odd turns the plot could take, and none of them made the slightest sense to me. I realized much later that she was just trying to get me thinking, doing what she could to

trigger my own auctorial imagination, but at the time I concluded that the woman was crazy. I wasn't quite sure what she
wanted me to do, but whatever it was, I didn't see how I could
do it.

So Henry put the book in a drawer, and that was that.

And then the day came when Henry told me he thought he
could sell *Sinner Man* to Irwin Stein at Lancer Books. I'd have
to enhance a couple of the sex scenes a bit, and I'd probably
want to slap a pen name on it, but I could get a few bucks for
the thing. A thousand? Fifteen hundred? Probably something
like that.

I'm not sure exactly when this took place. It would have to
have been at least a year after the debacle with Lee Wright, but
before the spring of 1964, when I had a falling out with the
Scott Meredith agency and they dropped me as a client. That's
not a very big window, but maybe *Sinner Man* could have slipped
through it.

Or else it would have been in 1966 or -7, by which time Henry
had split with Scott and set up on his own and I'd become his
client. "Remember *Sinner Man*? Do you happen to have a copy
around? Because I think I can sell it to Irwin Stein." That's how
the conversation might have gone.

Whenever it was, I was fine with it, and performed whatever
sexing up the book required, and cashed whatever check came
my way. I just hope I drank up the money, instead of pissing it
away on food and clothing.

Now here's my question:

What the hell happened to the book?

I never saw a copy. That's not as remarkable as it may sound,
because I hardly ever received author's copies of the books I
wrote back in the day. I went to stores often enough that I was

able to pick up a copy of most of them. (Well, two copies; I'd strip one of them and mount the cover on my office wall.) But I never saw this one, and would have had trouble finding it, because I never knew what title it was published under, and now can't even be sure what pen name I hung on it.

I *think* I used Sheldon Lord, which was a name I tacked on to my efforts for Midwood and Beacon. (I was reluctant to acknowledge this pen name for years, although it was a pretty open secret, because not all Sheldon Lord books are my work. I used ghostwriters—not for Midwood, I don't think, but definitely for Beacon, and three or four different gentlemen took a turn playing Sheldon Lord for that firm. (Similarly, I leased out Andrew Shaw, my pen name for Nightstand.) I never had copies of the books my ghosts produced; when I found them on the racks, that's where I left them.)

Now the disappearance of *Sinner Man* wouldn't have kept me up nights, or even afternoons, but for the emergence of Charles Ardai's Hard Case Crime. Charles reprinted several of my early Gold Medal titles, including *Grifter's Game* and *The Girl With the Long Green Heart*, and then the two of us began looking for unacknowledged pseudonymous books of mine that might fit the Hard Case imprint. Charles published *Killing Castro* and *Lucky at Cards* and *A Diet of Treacle*, and one otherwise fine morning I remembered *Sinner Man*.

And searched for it. Searched all the Internet used-book sites, searched hard for a Lancer title by Sheldon Lord. There weren't any—but there were two books listed, *Lust Couples* and *The Hours of Rapture*, both published by Domino Books in 1966, and Domino was a Lancer imprint. There was no way *Sinner Man* could have morphed into *Lust Couples*, but there must have been a few minutes of rapture within its pages, so a little poetic license seemed a possibility. I sent for *The Hours of Rapture*, and what turned up in the mailbox was a lesbian novel, one of the handful published in America that I hadn't written. I read enough to be sure it wasn't mine—a page, I think it took—and I tossed it aside. It was a book made to be tossed aside.

Here's what I think happened: after Scott and I parted ways, he went on submitting books by some of my ghosts, and some of them got published under one of my names. The pub date would certainly fit that scenario, and so would the fellow's past performance charts.

But what happened to *Sinner Man*? Did Lancer ever publish it, under some other title and pen name? They paid me for it, so they must have done something with it. And, if I had it back, well, Charles could publish it. I might make another thousand dollars, or even fifteen hundred. 2010 dollars, not 1967 dollars, but still.

So here's my question. Have you—yes, that would be *you*, Gentle Reader—have you read the book I described? Guy in Connecticut kills his wife, hops on a train, winds up in Buffalo, hooks up with the local mob, Berman included. Ring any bells?

Here's an incentive, okay? The first person to come up with the book will get, well, something. I could dedicate the book to you, say. Or, if you prefer, use your name for one of the characters. Or help your kid get into Antioch. Or, well, there must be something I can do for you.

Sheesh, if nobody can find the damn thing, I could always try writing it again. Hey, there's an idea. Now if only I could find Lee Wright's notes…

* * *

It was Don Marquis, whose *archie and mehitabel* verses did almost as much as e.e. cummings to dissuade young poets from the use of capital letters, who observed that publishing a volume of verses is like dropping a rose petal into the Grand Canyon and waiting for the echo.

This was a little bit different. My blog post got reprinted with enthusiasm on a few other websites, so there was a slight echo, but it proved a hollow sound indeed.

Nothing. No one remembered anything about the book. And I did a little more futile searching, and concluded that I couldn't find *Sinner Man* because it didn't exist. I knew I'd sold it to Lancer, but they didn't seem ever to have published it, and that sort of thing can and does happen. Publishers now and then wind up with manuscripts in inventory that never make it into print.

(That very nearly happened with the first three Matthew Scudder novels, truth to tell. Dell had real problems in the middle 1970s, and a lot of manuscripts they'd paid for were returned regretfully to their authors. If editor Bill Grose hadn't been such a staunch champion of the books, that might have been Scudder's fate. But I digress…)

So. I found other things to brood about, and that would have been that, if a Facebook friend of mine, Chris Gunter, hadn't tagged me in a photo he posted of half a dozen early books by Sheldon Lord.

Here's the exchange that followed:

James Miklasevich OK, where'd they come from? This is great.

Chris Gunter All these titles were from different book sellers across the United States. I always keep an eye out for gems like these.

Gerald Spannraft congrats I have about 100 of the paperbacks that were written under Shaw, Dexter and Lord. Block said many young writers used those names but some are definitely his.

Lawrence Block Chris, I see *Savage Lover* is noted as being first published in 1968. My last book as Sheldon Lord—and my last for that publisher—would have been 1964, 1965 at the latest. Two possibilities—this is somebody else's book—most likely— or an earlier one of mine under a new title. (Though if it's that good, maybe I should just accept it as my own and reissue it…)

Lawrence Block While I'm here, I should mention that three of these titles, *Community of Women*, *A Strange Kind of Love*, and *Warm and Willing*, are eVailable.

Chris Gunter Lawrence Block, it matches the description of the book you mention in *Write For Your Life* Chapter 3 page 34 SPOILER ALERT "I wrote a suspense novel about a man who kills his wife accidentally. He leaves town, surfaces in another city and creates a new identity for himself as a professional criminal, and manages to get taken up by the local mob, gradually becoming the hardened criminal he has pretended to be." Although that description might oversimplify this thrilling novel a bit, It's the exact same plot to a tee. Don the male protagonist becomes gangster Nat Crowley if those character names ring a bell.

Lawrence Block Wow! I've been searching for that one for years, never able to run it down. My title was *Sinner Man*, and I thought it had been sold—finally—years after it was written, but never could find it. I ordered it earlier today from ABEBooks, and a copy's en route; if it's the book—and it sounds as though it must be—I'll probably contrive to publish it, ideally with Hard Case Crime. (Hear that, Charles Ardai?)

Chris Gunter I'd be remiss if I didn't mention my good friend John Gilbert, I purchased my first copy of this novel from his book store Books Galore. I had just finished reading *Girl With the Long Green Heart* and *A Diet of Treacle* back to back and was convinced *Savage Lover* had to be one of your novels.

Lawrence Block Yeah, that's it, *Sinner Man*. He wound up in Buffalo, right? Nat Crowley indeed. I'll be a son of a bitch.

Charles Ardai I hear, I hear! Can't wait to read it!

Amazing. I'd found the book—not through the 2010 post on the Mulholland blog, but from something I'd written all the way back in 1985.

That was when I wrote and self-published *Write For Your Life,* a book version of the interactional seminar for writers my wife and I had developed. The book had been sufficiently successful to go quickly out of print, and the miracle of Print-on-Demand publishing had since made it feasible to return it to print in early 2014.

Until Chris Gunter quoted the book on Facebook, I'd long since forgotten that I'd recounted the story of *Sinner Man* therein. And why wouldn't I? I'd told the tale thirty years ago—of a book that by then was a quarter century old.

Never mind. Two copies of *Sinner Man*, in the guise of *Savage Lover*, arrived within the week, and a single glance confirmed what the Facebook exchange had already assured me. This was my book, that once was lost and now was found.

And it was easy to see why I'd been unable to find it earlier. The publisher, whose little lighthouse logo appears in the book's upper left corner, was Softcover Library. And, you'll recall, I'd been dead certain it was Lancer Books.

Now I'd written for Softcover Library (also known occasionally as Beacon Books—hence the lighthouse—and Universal Publishing & Distributing). They'd published three early Sheldon Lord titles, *Community of Women, April North,* and *Pads are for Passion.*

(*Community of Women* was their title and their idea, and came to me as an assignment. They liked it enough to ask me to write something else, and liked *April North* enough to keep my title. *Pads are for Passion* was not written with them in mind; it drew on aspects of Greenwich Village life I wanted to treat fictionally, and I'd hoped for a better publisher, but when several houses passed my agent sent it to Beacon/Softcover/Universal. I wasn't hugely surprised when they changed the title, as I'd called it *A Diet of Treacle,* and hardly expected to find that title on a book with a little lighthouse in the upper left corner.)

Then, for a couple of years in the early 1960s, Softcover published a whole run of books by Sheldon Lord—but I didn't write them, and in fact never even read them. I was still represented by Scott Meredith, and when Softcover asked for more of Sheldon Lord, someone at Scott's office dug up a ghostwriter to turn out the books. I contributed nothing to this venture but my name, and received $200 per book for it. That doesn't sound like a lot of money now, and in fact it wasn't a whole lot of money then, either, but it came in handy.

When Scott Meredith and I split the blanket in 1964, I had a book in hand. It was about a card sharp, and I called it *Lucky at Cards,* and tried to figure out what to do with it. I sent it unagented to Softcover, and they published it as *The Sex Shuffle.* (Hard Case Crime has since reissued it under its original title.)

And that was my last book for that publisher.

They were, I must tell you, ghastly to work with in one respect. The publisher, an elderly fellow named Abramson, had certain basic convictions, and one was that all manuscripts had to be edited substantially in order to be publishable. As a result, the fool had half a dozen people on staff whose job it was to put a great many pencil marks on every page of manuscript that passed over their desks.

So they would take two simple sentences and make a compound sentence out of them, and in the next paragraph they'd take a compound sentence and break it into two simple ones. For no apparent reason—other than that they wanted to keep their jobs.

I found this out when I got a copy of either *April North* or *Community of Women* and read the first couple of pages. Right away I hit a sentence that struck me as awfully clunky, and wondered how I could have written it. Then I hit another just as bad, and retrieved my carbon copy of the book from the closet shelf. (I kept a carbon copy of everything until the book was published, at which time I felt free to discard it.)

And no, those clunky sentences weren't mine. The same weirdness prevailed throughout the book, and when I brought all of this to agent Henry Morrison's attention, he explained Mr. Abramson's editorial policy.

Ah well.

The point (he said, brushing away a tear) is that I didn't think a great deal of Softcover Library, or Beacon, or whatever you want to call them. And when Henry was representing me again, after he too had taken leave of Scott Meredith and set up his own shop, he remembered *Sinner Man,* and had me augment its sexual aspect with a scene here and another scene there, and sent it off to my old friends at Beacon/Softcover. And I got whatever I got ($1000? $1500?) and turned my attention to other things.

And never heard anything more about the book, and remembered it as having been sold not to Beacon but to Irwin Stein at Lancer Books. I was writing a variety of books for Irwin, and it would certainly have made sense to lay off *Sinner Man* with him, and that's what I managed to believe had happened.

Thus, if I ever ran across a copy of *Savage Lover,* or encountered it in a list of books, I'd have passed it by without a second thought, dismissing it as one of the dozen Sheldon Lord books written by ghostwriters. If I'd even noticed the 1968 pub date, I'd have concluded that the publisher had, not for the first time, reissued an early book with or without a cover and title change, or—also not for the first time—that Scott Meredith, old pirate that he was, had set some other ghost to operating under my pen name, even though we'd parted company four years earlier.

Well, that's all more than you needed to know, isn't it? But I always enjoyed listening to Paul Harvey, and the best part of each broadcast was when he'd intone, "And now, the rest of the story."

When *Sinner Man* finally came my way in the guise of *Savage Lover,* it needed work. Elements of the first chapter bothered me, and I decided to rewrite the opening. And Charles took on the thankless task (though that may be an inappropriate adjective, as I thank him all the time) of line-editing the text, cleaning up Beacon's bad editorial choices and my own infelicitous phrases and never knowing which was which.

And Charles had a couple of questions, which I answered to his satisfaction. But they might well have occurred to you as well, so why don't I repeat them and answer them here?

Was it really that simple to get a Social Security card in the early 1960s? Didn't you have to show identification?

Yes, it was really that simple. It would have been the mid-1950s when I got my card, and all I did was take the bus downtown to the appropriate government office and fill out a form. The card I was given said right on it "Not to be Used for

Identification Purposes," and I can see why, because they gave it to me without my having to make even a token effort to prove who I was.

I think I went back another time to pick one up for my friend Tom Manford.

Who?

Oh, right, I never told you about him. During my junior year in high school, I acquired a new wallet, either bought it myself or got it as a gift. Either way, it came with a couple of cards in it, one a piece of dummy ID in the name of Thomas B. Manford. So over the next few months I picked up other pieces of ID for Tom, including a Social Security card.

It was harmless enough, and did provide a small amount of amusement at school, where Thomas Manford managed to get on a few lists, and occasionally failed to respond to a roll call. And, late in my senior year, when the elections of class officers were held, a few of us got the word out. For Class Historian, we told everybody, vote for Tom Manford. Most kids just nodded dutifully; those who asked who the hell Manford was were quickly assured that he was a really great guy, and he'd do a hell of a job.

Well, he won. And the results were quickly thrown out, and a new election held. I believe my friend Richard Dattner won this time, and I'm sure he did a hell of a job with the History of Bennett High's Class of 1955, probably even better than anything Manford might have managed.

Richard's an architect now, a very distinguished one. I don't know what ever became of Tom Manford. Jesus, come to think of it, he's old enough to be collecting Social Security…

If so, I bet he has to show ID. It's hard to believe it was that easy to get a Social Security card. Maybe it was different in Buffalo.

Well, Buffalo's where I got my card, and Tom Manford's, too. And, since it's where Nat Crowley got his, it hardly matters how they did it in the rest of the country. But I checked with my Frequent Companion, who grew up in New Orleans, and she confirmed that was how it worked in the Crescent City in the early 1960s. You walked in, you told them your name, and they gave you a card.

And yes, it's hard to believe nowadays. Just yesterday I went to a midtown medical office in Madison Avenue, and I had to provide a thumbprint and a semen sample just to get access to the building. Upstairs they wanted to see a driver's license, and took my palm print and photograph so that no future impostor could pass himself off as me and filch urine specimens.

Okay, I guess I believe you about the Social Security card. But what about the train?

Yes, they still had trains then. I know it's hard to believe, but trains ran with some frequency between American cities, and passengers rode them, and—

I'm talking about the toilets on trains. Did they really flush right onto the tracks?

They did.

I mean, nowadays they flush into a tank, and it's emptied at the end of the run, but in the book—

It took them awhile to come up with the idea of a receiving tank for waste. They certainly didn't have it in Nat Crowley's day. And each lavatory bore a cautionary sign, enjoining one against so fouling the trackbed within a station:

> *"Passengers will please refrain*
> *from flushing toilets while the train*
> *is passing through the station."*

It's poetry in motion, isn't it? I mean it could even be haiku, but with a few extra syllables.

More of a song lyric, I'd say, and it was in fact commonly sung to the tune of Dvorak's *Humoresque*. One appended the words "I love you" to fill out the last three notes of the melody. But don't take my word for it. Oscar Brand's full version is easily found on YouTube, and worth a listen.

WANT MORE BLOCK?

If you enjoyed SINNER MAN,
the very first crime novel by
LAWRENCE BLOCK,
you'll love his latest

THE GIRL WITH THE DEEP BLUE EYES

available now from your favorite
local or online bookseller.

Read on for a sample...

ONE

The phone woke him from a dream. At first his dream simply incorporated the sound in its narrative, and his dream-hand picked it up and his dream-voice said hello, and there his imagination quit on him, failing to invent a caller on the other end of the line. He said hello again, and the real-world phone went on ringing, and he shook off the dream and got the phone from the bedside table.

"Hello?"

"Doak Miller?"

"Right," he said. "Who's this?"

"Susie at the Sheriff's Office. Sorry, your voice sounded different."

"Thick with sleep."

"Oh, did I wake you? I'm sorry. Do you want to call us back?"

"No, it's what? Close to nine-thirty, time I was up. What can I do for you?"

"Um—"

"So long as it's not too complicated."

"On account of you're still not completely awake?"

He'd gotten a smile out of her, could hear it in her voice. He could picture her at her desk, twirling a strand of yellow hair around her finger, happy to let a phone conversation turn a little bit flirty.

"Oh, I'm awake," he said. "Just not at the absolute top of my game."

"Well, do you figure you're sharp enough for me to put you through to Sheriff Bill?"

"He won't be using a lot of big words, will he?"

"I'll warn him not to," she said. "You hold now, hear?"

Just the least bit flirty, because it was safe to flirt with him, wasn't it? He was old enough to be her father, old enough to be *retired*, for God's sake.

He let that thought go and went back for a look at his dream, but all that was left of it was the ringing telephone with no one on the other end of it. If the phone hadn't rung, he'd have awakened with no recollection of having dreamt. He knew he dreamed, knew everyone did, but he never remembered his dreams, or even that his sleep had been anything other than an uninterrupted void.

It was as if he led two lives, a sleeping life and a waking life, and it took the interruption of a phone call to make one life bleed through into the other.

"Doak?"

"Sheriff," he said. "How may I serve the good people of Gallatin County?"

"Now that's what I ask myself every hour of every day. You'll never believe the answer came back to me first thing this morning."

"Try me."

"'Hire a hit man.'"

"So you thought of me."

"You know, there must be another fellow with your qualifications between Tampa and Panama City, but I wouldn't know how to get him on the phone. Susie said you were sleeping when she called, but you sound wide awake to me. You want to come by once you've had your breakfast?"

"Have y'all got coffee?"

"I'll tell her to make a fresh pot," Sheriff William Radburn said. "In your honor, sir."

✲

When he'd moved to the state three years ago, Doak had put up at first in a motel just across the Taylor County line. A Gujarati family owned it, and the office smelled not unpleasantly of curry. It took him a couple of months to tire of the noise of the other guests and the small-screen TV, and he let a housewife with a real estate license show him some houses. The one he liked was off by itself, with a dock on a creek that flowed into the gulf. You could hitch a boat to that dock, she'd pointed out. Or you could fish right off the dock.

He made an offer. When the owner accepted it, the agent delivered the good news in person. He'd had a beer going, and offered her one. She hesitated just long enough to signal that her acceptance was significant.

"Well," he said. "How are we going to celebrate?"

She gave him a look, and that was answer enough, but to underscore the look she twisted the wedding ring off her finger and dropped it in her purse. Then she looked at him again.

Her name was Barb—"Like a fishhook," she'd said—and while she wasn't the first woman he'd been to bed with since the move south, she was the first to join him in his room at the Gulf Mirage Motel. What better way, really, to celebrate his departure than by nailing the woman who'd facilitated it?

And she had a nice enough body, built more for comfort than for speed. Her breasts were nice, her ass was even nicer, and long before she'd shown him the house he wound up buying, he'd already decided not only that he wanted her but just how he intended to have her.

So when he went down on her he got a finger in her ass, and while she tensed up at first she wound up going with it. Her orgasm was a strong one, and had barely ended when he rolled her over and arranged her on her knees. He moistened himself in her pussy, and she was so warm and wet he had to force himself to leave, but he withdrew and she gave a little gasp at his departure and another when she felt him where his finger had been earlier.

She said, "Oh, I don't think—"

It wasn't much of a protest and he didn't pay any attention to it, forcing himself into her, feeling her resist, feeling her resistance subside, feeling her open for him only to tighten around him. He fucked her gently at first, then more savagely as passion took hold of him, and he cried out as he emptied himself into her.

He went away someplace for a moment, and the next thing he was aware of was lying on his back while she cleansed him with a washcloth. "Just a tame little thing now," she said, "but it like to split me in two a few minutes ago."

She took him in her mouth, and for an hour or so they found things to do. Then he got two more beers from the mini-fridge and they sat up in bed drinking them.

She said, "I hardly ever like that."

"Sex?"

"Silly. No, you know. Butt sex."

"You got into it pretty good there."

"I almost came. Which is something I never did."

"Came that way?"

"Never even enjoyed it, not really. I wonder if I ever could come that way."

"From getting fucked in the ass?"

"That sounds so *dirty*. Saying butt sex is bad enough."

"With an ass like yours—"

"I saw the way you looked at it. I knew what you wanted to do." She looked at him over the top of the beer can, weighed her words carefully. "I knew you wanted to fuck me in my ass."

"Your gorgeous ass."

"My gorgeous ass. My gorgeous ass which is a little sore, but I'm not complaining. I thought, oh, that's what he's gonna want to do, I just know it."

"And you hardly ever like it."

"And yet," she said, "I took my ring off, didn't I? Which reminds me." She got the ring from her purse, put it on her finger. "Now I'm married again," she said. "And I'm in desperate need of a shower. It's bad enough I'll be going home smelling of beer."

She showered, toweled dry. While she was dressing he went over and put his hands on her, but she said, "No, not now. And you can finish my beer for me, because I've had enough, and what I have to do now is stop at Cozy Cole's for my usual end-of-the-day glass of Chardonnay."

"So you can smell of wine instead of beer."

"Probably a little of both," she said, "with a top note of—no, never mind. Doak? We're not going to have a romance, are we?"

"No."

"No, we're not, which means we can probably do this every now and then without worrying that it'll blow up in our faces. But maybe I'm getting ahead of myself here. I mean, would you want to do this every now and then? Like maybe a couple of times a month?"

"I'd like that."

"Like friends with benefits, I guess they call it, except I don't even know that we'd be friends. Friendly, sure, but friends?"

"Just so we get the benefits."

"And I'd be interested in finding out if I can come that way."

TWO

It turned out she could. They established as much on her first
visit to his new house, and it was a few days after that momen-
tous occasion that he paid his first visit to the Gallatin County
sheriff's office. It was a courtesy call, and a counterpart to one
he'd made to the Taylor County sheriff not long after the state
of Florida had licensed him as a private investigator. He didn't
even know how much use he'd get out of the license, he could
get by easily enough on his NYPD pension, but it never hurt to
be on good terms with the local law, and he'd known retired
cops back home with P. I. tickets who picked up the occasional
piece of work through friends still on the job.

The sheriff of Taylor County turned out to be a piece of
work himself, a slick article with a college diploma framed on
his wall, and enough of a cracker accent to establish his bona
fides as a good old boy. Doak could tell the man had an eye on
the state house in Tallahassee, along with a snowball's chance
of getting there, but he was young enough that it'd be another
five years before he figured out that last part. Sheriff D. T.
Newton was cordial enough, because he'd never be less than
cordial to anyone without a reason, but Doak could tell right
away they were never going to be Best Friends Forever.

The Gallatin County courtesy call was a good deal more
fruitful. Bill Radburn was a genuine good old boy who didn't
feel the need to act like one. If he'd ever had ambitions for
higher office, he'd shed them somewhere along the way, and
now all he wanted was to do his job well enough to keep the
voters happy. His age was around sixty to Doak's forty-eight,

and he liked ESPN and his wife's cooking, and the photo cube
on his desk showed pictures of his grandchildren.

"Retired from the NYPD," he'd said. "Put in your twenty
years?"

"Closer to twenty-five."

"And Tallahassee saw fit to give you a private license, though
it's hard to guess what it'll do for you here in Gallatin County.
Though I guess you never know, given the tendency folks have
to get themselves in messes they can't get out of on their own."

"Oh, they do that down here, do they?"

"Now and again," the sheriff said.

And Doak had found occasion to drop in now and again himself, to drink a cup of coffee and swap war stories in a way he'd
never have tried with D. T. Newton. Folks did get in messes,
and now and then one of them turned up on his doorstep, and he
got to pick up an honest fee for a little honest work. Sometimes
he had to drive around, sometimes he had to talk to people, but
a surprising amount of the time he got the job done and made
the client happy without leaving his desk. More often than
you'd guess, your computer could go around and knock on doors
for you—and did it all without pissing off the person on the
other side of the door.

None of his clients ever came to him through Bill Radburn.
But then one day his phone rang, and half an hour later he was
in the man's office on Citrus Boulevard. He'd said he'd done
undercover work now and again, hadn't he? Well, here they
were looking at a local fellow who very likely knew everybody
with a badge within a fifty-mile radius, and he hated to call in
the staties in Tallahassee if he didn't have to. So was he up for a
little exercise in role-playing?

And the following afternoon he was sitting in his beat-up
Monte Carlo in the parking lot of the Winn-Dixie, settling into

the role of a mobbed-up hit man from northern New Jersey—
"Bergen County, maybe you's heard of it"—agreeing to rid a
man with the second most profitable auto dealership in Gallatin
County of his business partner.

"He won't buy me out, he won't let me buy *him* out, and I
can't stand the sight of the son of a bitch," the man said. "So
what choice do I have here?"

"The man has a point," Radburn said, when they listened to
the recording of the conversation. They played it again for the
District Attorney, Pierce Weldon, whose vision of the future
was not limited to Gallatin County, and who clearly liked what
he was hearing.

"How's a man that stupid sell so many cars?" he wondered.
"Jesus, the dumb bastard lays it all out there in black and white,
or it will be when it's typed up. Though credit where it's due,
Mr. Doak."

"Just Doak," Radburn said. "Last name's Miller."

"My mistake, but all the same, Doak, I have to say you make
a very convincing hit man. I damn near bought your act myself.
I don't suppose you ever crossed the street to do a little moon-
lighting, did you?"

"If I did," he said, "I wouldn't say so. Be just my luck you'd
be wearing a wire."

They all assumed he'd have to testify, but the auto dealer's
attorney listened to the tape a couple of times and convinced
his client to plead guilty. After sentencing, Doak and Radburn
and Weldon shook hands all around. "And another solid citizen
wins himself a ticket to Raiford," the D.A. said. "That trophy
wife of his was all teary-eyed, but I don't guess she'll have too
much trouble finding somebody to elevate her spirits. Won't be
me, I know that much, and I'd like to think it's my high moral
principles but it may just be cowardice."

"They do dress alike," Radburn said, "and it can be tricky to tell them apart."

"And it won't be you either, Grandfather William, because you're just too damned comfortable with your life as it is to reinvent yourself as Foxy Grandpa. But our cop-turned-hit man might find an opening here, so to speak. You're not married, are you, Doak?"

"Used to be."

"Was that a note of bitterness there? And you live alone? No entangling alliances? But maybe your sensitive self recoils at the idea of literally doing unto the wife what you've already done metaphorically to the husband."

"I did that once," he remembered.

"Oh?"

"Guy was a burglar, caught him before he could get the goods to a fence."

"And he had a hot wife?"

He nodded. "I knew better, but…"

"So many sad stories start with those four words."

"This wasn't that sad because it didn't last that long. She liked her booze, and after the third drink something in her eyes would change, and I realized I was afraid to fall asleep in her bed for fear that she'd stick a knife in me."

"Or go all Lorena Bobbitt on you."

"Jesus, there's a name from the past. Which is probably where it should stay."

And he knew he wouldn't hit on the auto dealer's wife, either. Because he was capable of learning from experience.

Besides, hell, she wasn't *that* hot.

THREE

The coffee Susie poured him was fresh, though not as strong as he'd have preferred. He settled in his chair across the desk from the sheriff and asked just who it was who wanted to dissolve a partnership.

"It's not like that this time," Radburn said, and stopped himself. "Except, come to think of it, it is."

"How's that?"

"Wife wants you to kill her husband," he said. "So it's a partnership, but of the domestic persuasion."

"And she wants me—"

"Well, not specifically, since she doesn't know you. At least I hope she doesn't, because that would be a deal breaker, wouldn't it? She's expecting a dead-eyed assassin, and who shows up but her buddy Doak from the Tuesday Night Bowling League."

"Wouldn't work."

"Her name's Lisa Otterbein, but her maiden name's Yarrow, and that's what she uses professionally. And I suspect she'll go back to it altogether once you kill George Otterbein for her."

"And we know she wants me to do this because—"

"Because three nights ago she sat down across a table from a fellow named Richard Lyle Gonson. Know him?"

"I don't think so."

"If you were looking to hire a hit man, he'd be a natural to sit across the table from. Not because you think he'd take the job, but because he'd probably know somebody who would. Or somebody who'd know somebody."

"He's not Reverend R. L. Gonson, the Congregationalist minister."

Radburn shook his head. "He's done, as the saying goes, a little of this and a little of that. He mostly gets away with it, but he's done a few bids, one of them federal. It's getting on for ten years since the last time he got out."

"He's behaving himself?"

"Does the bear give up a lifelong habit of sylvan defecation? Best he can do is learn to cover it up afterward. Even so, I had him for receiving last year, right around the end of hurricane season."

"But you couldn't make it stick?"

"He had something to trade."

"Ah."

"That's one way to cover up the pile in the woods. We got the chance to put away somebody who'd been giving us a lot more grief than Mr. Gonson ever did, and he saw the wisdom of having friends in law enforcement. So when Lisa let him know what she wanted, instead of telling her to go shit in her hat—"

"Or in the woods."

"—he said he knew the very man to call."

"And that man turned out to be you."

"It did. Neither of those names ring a bell? George Otterbein? Lisa Yarrow Otterbein?"

He shook his head.

"George's father started a restaurant-supply business. George inherited it and married money. Made a good thing of the business and invested some of the proceeds in local real estate. Rental properties, mostly, bringing in more money to go with the money he's already got."

"I'm guessing Lisa's a second wife."

"You New Yorkers, nothing gets past you. First wife was in one of those fifty-car chain pile-ups on 41. Foggy morning and one guy stops short and everybody hits him. Airbag deployed and Jo was unhurt, but somebody insisted she go to the hospital as a precaution, and while they were checking her they found something they didn't like, and so they checked some more, and she had cancer cells in everything but her hair."

"Jesus."

"Two months later she was gone. No symptoms before the accident, and it's hard not to think that if they hadn't found it she'd still be alive today. Which is ridiculous, but still."

Nothing to say to that. Doak sipped his coffee.

"You know the Cattle Baron? On Camp Road a mile or so north of Lee?"

"I've passed it. Never stopped."

"That'd be the best policy if you chanced to be a vegetarian. Just hold your breath and drive on by. Steak and seafood's what they've got on offer, and the steak's dry-aged prime Angus beef. After he buried Jo, George got in the habit of taking his dinners at the Baron. He was partial to their bone-in rib eye, which I can recommend, assuming you're not a vegetarian."

"I'll have to try it."

"You might want to wait a couple of weeks. All goes well, they'll have to find somebody new to show you to your table."

"Lisa's the hostess?"

"She showed George to his table every night, and I guess that wasn't all she showed him, and as soon as Jo was six months in the ground they went and got married. He'd had three children with Jo, two girls and a boy, and the oldest was the same age as Lisa. Now there's different ways kids will react to that sort of thing. Either the new wife's an angel for offering their daddy a second chance for happiness, or she's a gold-digging bitch. My experience, the more money's involved, the less likely she is to get the benefit of the doubt."

"Figures. She kept her job after they got married?"

Radburn shook his head. "Moved into his big house on Rumsey Road and set about being a woman of leisure. Spent some of George's money redecorating, bought some antiques in Tampa and some art in Miami. That held her interest for the better part of two years, and then she turned up one night back at the Cattle Baron, greeting her old customers by name and showing them to their tables like she'd never left."

"And the marriage?"

"I guess the honeymoon was over. If Lisa was working evenings, that had to cut into their together time. Far as anyone knew, they were comfortable enough with the new arrangement."

"Until a couple of nights ago."

"Until a couple of nights ago, when Rich Gonson and two other fellows came by to eat some meat and drink some whiskey. When Lisa brought the check to the table, she told him to stick around."

"And he did."

"Thought he was about to get lucky, according to him, but after his friends left and she sat down at his table, our girl was all business. 'Of course I don't know anybody in that line of work,' he told me—"

"Meaning he does."

"Wouldn't surprise me. What he told Lisa was he'd have to make a few phone calls, and the first call he made was to me. So last night I told Mary Beth she was about due for dinner out, and we had us a couple of shrimp cocktails and split the big rib eye, and I paid the tab myself instead of expensing it to Gallatin County."

"What a guy."

"Left a good tip, too. And took a picture when no one was paying attention." He found the photo on his iPhone, handed it across the desk. "Lisa Yarrow Otterbein."

"Very nice."

"She had long hair when she married George. I don't know when she got it cut, but it was short like that by the time she was back working at the Baron. I understand a woman's trying to tell you something when she cuts her hair, but they never gave me the code book. You ever seen her before? That you remember?"

He shook his head. "I'd remember," he said.

"Then she's probably never met you, either, so there's no reason she won't believe you're Frankie from New Jersey. Of course, the accent may give you away. You're starting to talk Southern."

"I am?"

"On the phone this morning. 'Have y'all got coffee?' That how they'd say it in Jersey?"

"Maybe South Jersey." He took another look at Lisa Otterbein's picture. Lisa Otterbein, Lisa Yarrow, whatever she called herself. The haircut, he decided, was probably a good idea, whatever the psychological motivation behind it. The short hair drew attention to her facial features, and it was a face you wanted to study. Beautiful, but that was almost beside the point.

"Give me your email, why don't you, and I'll send you the photo. Otherwise I get the feeling I'll never get my phone back."

FOUR

Back at his house, he set up a folding chair on the dock and sat there looking out through the mangroves. He hadn't bought a boat, hadn't even considered it, but one afternoon he'd stopped at a tackle shop and let the kid sell him enough basic gear so that he could bait a hook and drop a line in the water.

He'd tried that once, spent an hour or two on his dock, and whatever disappointment he'd felt in failing to haul in a fish was outweighed by his relief at not having to clean and cook his catch. The rod and reel were in his garage, along with the tackle box, and he'd never had the urge to repeat the experiment. But the dock was a nice place to hang out, as long as you didn't screw it up with a boat or a fishing rod.

He'd brought a magazine out onto the dock with him, but paid little attention to it. When he wasn't gazing off into the middle distance, letting his mind wander, he was looking at the photo the sheriff had sent him. Lisa, with her face framed by feather-cut dark hair.

A full-lipped mouth, but not overly so. Visible cheekbones, a pointy chin that just missed being sharp. Big eyes, accented with mascara, and what color were they, anyway? It was a good picture, but you couldn't tell the color of her eyes.

He could feel the fantasy, hovering out there on the edge of thought.

When had it first come to him? Maybe four, five years into his marriage. By then he'd already let go of his marriage vows, or at least the one about forsaking all others. He didn't go out chasing other women, but when the opportunity came along and the chemistry was right, he let it happen.

It wasn't the worst marriage in the world, but it never should have happened in the first place. He'd tried college and when that didn't work for him he went into the service. It was the peacetime army, and he'd finished his hitch and come home well before Operation Desert Storm and the Gulf War. A buddy was going to take the exam to get on the cops, so he went with him and passed, and went through the academy and came out with a gun and a badge and a stick.

And a uniform, in which he felt terribly self-conscious. But everybody did at first, and everybody got over it.

He met Doreen at a party. She had a cop for a brother, but nobody he knew. They started keeping company, and he was beginning to think it was time to break up with her when she told him she was pregnant. "Look, it's not the end of the world," she said. "I mean, we love each other, right? So we'd be getting married sooner or later anyway, wouldn't we?"

No, he thought, and no. He didn't love her and they wouldn't be getting married anyway. But what he said was, "Yeah, I guess you're right. When you look at it that way."

And it wasn't horrible. There were things he liked about being married. And he loved his son when he was born, and the daughter who followed a year and a half later.

Or did he? He figured he must, because you were supposed to.

So he cheated, when something came along, but he didn't chase, and it seemed to him that the cheating made it easier to stay married. Made life a little more interesting. The job was interesting, and the uniform no longer made him feel self-conscious, and anyway he was on track for a move into plainclothes. If the marriage wasn't interesting, well, the occasional vacation from it made it more tolerable.

The fantasy: *He meets this woman, and their eyes lock, and they connect in a way that neither of them has ever before connected with another human being.*

And that's just it, because they walk out of their separate lives and into a life together. Not a word to anybody, not a wasted moment to pack a bag or quit a job. They look at each other, and they connect, and they're in a car riding off together, or on a bus or a train or an airplane, and it's crazy and they know it's crazy but they don't care.

Of course it never happened. He met women, and now and then there was a connection, and sometimes it led as far as a bedroom, but it was never the magic mystical connection of the fantasy. Once or twice he thought he might be in love, and maybe he was, for a little while. And then he wasn't.

There was one woman—Cathy, her name was—and he imagined being married to her instead of Doreen. He could see her in that role, and he thought about it, and then one day he realized that he was able to envision her taking Doreen's place because she was in fact very like Doreen. And if the two of them wound up together, they'd just recreate the marriage he already had with Doreen. He'd be in the same place, and in short order he'd be cheating on Cathy, too, and the only difference would be the checks he'd be writing every month for alimony and child support.

There was no alimony in the fantasy, no child support either. That was because there was no past in the fantasy, no tin cans tied to the bumper of whatever vehicle whisked them away, him and his fantasy partner, into a wholly desirable if equally unimaginable future.

Well, that was fantasy for you.

Instead, he was stuck with the reality of a marriage that limped along. He was used to it, and he assumed Doreen was used to it, too, and then he went through a rough patch on the job, and that was working itself out, more or less, and Doreen surprised him by filing for divorce.

Nasty divorce, too. The boy was in college and the girl in her last year in high school, and they were young enough to think they had to take sides, and it was no contest, the side they took was their mother's.

Well, okay.

He could have retired when he had twenty years in, that was what a lot of guys did, but he'd always liked the job more than he'd disliked it, and your pension was better if you hung around for twenty-five. So he'd planned on doing that, and then Doreen did what she did, and all he wanted was to kiss everything goodbye.

It was like the fantasy, sort of, except there was nobody sharing it. Just his own middle-aged self and two mismatched suitcases, getting on a plane at JFK, getting off in Tampa. A night in a chain motel at the airport, then a cab to a used-car lot, where he'd paid cash for the Chevy Monte Carlo he was still driving. It would pass, as they said, everything but a gas station, but he led a low-mileage life and didn't mind what he spent on gas.

Then he'd pointed the car north. He'd been to Florida a few times over the years, mostly with Doreen. He wasn't sure where he wanted to be, but Tampa was too far south and the Panhandle was too far north, and when he got as far as Perry, in Taylor County, he thought it felt about right. He had dinner at Mindy's Barbecue and bedded down at the Ramada, and two nights later he moved to the Gulf Mirage to save a few bucks.

And so on.

A bird settled on a branch a few yards from him, then flew off. You could see a lot of birds from the dock, especially around sunrise and sunset. He couldn't tell one bird from another, but there were books, if he wanted to pursue the subject. And a pair of binoculars would make it easier to see what he was looking at.

And how long before the binoculars wound up in the garage, next to the fishing tackle?

He settled himself in his chair and let his eyes close, and the next thing he knew the phone was ringing.

"All set," Bill Radburn told him. "She'll come by the Winn-Dixie lot at half past eleven tomorrow morning. You'll be in a royal blue Chevy Monte Carlo parked all by itself at the rear of the lot. At least I think you will. You didn't cross me up by buying a new car, did you?"

"No, but it's closer to green than blue. I think it says 'teal' on the registration."

"Well, don't go run out now and get it painted. She'll be able to find you. I wondered about the Winn-Dixie, though. I had Susie check what made the papers the last time we did this, just to make sure they never mentioned where the sting went down. We're clear."

"Good."

"I guess. I checked with Motor Vehicles, and she'll probably be driving a silver-gray Lexus. But if she gets there before you, don't pull up next to her. Park off by yourself and let her come to you. I don't have to tell you why, do I?"

"So it's not entrapment?"

"That's the reasoning. Must have been worked out by some bright young fellow trained by the Jesuits. I'll tell you something, Doak. I know this isn't entrapment but I can't say it doesn't feel like it."

"She's the one who sat down with Gonson."

"Oh, she thought it up and brought it up, she's the one decided she'd rather be a real widow than a grass one. She's trying to arrange a murder, and we prevent that murder by sup-plying a fake killer for her to meet with. But if the whole point is to keep a murder from happening, shit, all I'd have to do is polish off another rib eye. When she comes over to the table, what I do is put my cards on it. 'I know what you've got in mind, sweetheart, and don't bother to deny it. And if anything happens to your husband, I'll know just who to look at. So you better either divorce him or pray he lives to be a hundred.' You care to tell me that wouldn't work?"

"It probably would."

"Damn right it would. She'd miss out on a few years in an orange jumpsuit and George would be spared knowing that his wife wanted him dead. And I'd be shirking my duty."

"Which is to lock up the bad guys."

"And girls, right. And if she'll go so far as to hire a killer, who's to say society is better off with her on the loose? I might be able to frighten her out of having George Otterbein killed, but would that scare some moral fiber into her?" A sigh. "So we'll play this by the book. Eleven-thirty in the Winn-Dixie lot. She'll be bringing a thousand dollars as earnest money, and it'd be best if you could get her to hand it to you."

"Understood."

"And you won't forget to wear a wire, will you?"

"What an idea."

"And remember you're a Jersey boy. You wouldn't want to slip and say something like, 'Bergen County, maybe y'all have heard of it.'"

He watched the local news, the national news. Five minutes of *Pardon the Interruption* on ESPN, five minutes of *Jeopardy*. Took a shower, decided he could get by without a shave, then changed his mind and shaved anyway.

Couldn't decide which shirt to wear. Crazy, he thought, and stupid in the bargain. He didn't have that many shirts, and nobody was going to notice what he was wearing, and it's not as though he was looking to make an impression.

Been a while since he'd had a good steak. No need to read more than that into it.

FIVE

And it was a good steak, no question about it, well-marbled and tender. The cliché about doughnuts notwithstanding, cops learned to eat well in New York, and at one time or another he'd had steak dinners at Keen's, Smith & Wollensky, and Peter Luger. If the Cattle Baron's rib eye wasn't the best he'd ever had, it was certainly in the top ten.

He ordered it black and blue, not sure if they'd know what that meant, and he wasn't reassured by the faint look of puzzlement on the face of the dishwater-blonde waitress. But she evidently passed the order on to a chef who knew what he had in mind, and his steak showed up charred on the outside and blood-rare within. It was a generous serving, accompanied by a baked potato and a side of creamed spinach, and it was almost enough to take his mind off Lisa Yarrow Otterbein.

Almost.

The fantasy, brought up to date:

He sits over a cup of coffee, watching her. She can't see him, but his gaze is strong enough for her to feel it, even though she doesn't know exactly what it is that she feels.

She approaches his table, asks him if everything is all right. He says it is.

But none of their words matter. Their eyes have locked together, and something passes between them, a current as impossible to identify as it is to deny.

She says her name: "Lisa. Lisa Yarrow."

"Doak Miller."

"We close at eleven. That's when I get off."

"But we don't have to wait until then, do we?"

"No, of course not. I'm through here. As soon as you finish your coffee—"

He puts money on the table. "I'm done with my coffee," he says.

He gets to his feet. She takes his arm. They walk through the dining room and out of the restaurant.

She points to her car.

"We'll take mine," he says.

"Good," she says. "His money bought it. I don't want it anymore."

He holds the door for her, walks around the car, gets behind the wheel. The car starts up right away, and he pulls out of the lot and heads north on Camp Road.

They drive for twenty minutes in silence. Eventually she asks him where they are going.

"Do you care?"

She thinks about it. "No," she says at length. "No, not at all."

The reality:

She comes to his table without being summoned, or even stared at. She asks him if everything was all right. He says it was.

Their eyes never meet.

The blonde waitress brings the check. He takes a credit card from his wallet, thinks better of it, puts it back. And, as in the fantasy, puts bills on the table.

Back home, he booted up his computer, checked his email, dropped in at a couple of websites. Found something to Google, and let one thing lead to another.

Running it all through his mind.

He thought about—and Googled—Karla Faye Tucker. Killed some people with a pickax during a 1983 robbery in Texas, got herself convicted and sentenced to death the following year, and executed by lethal injection in 1999. She found God in prison, which is where He evidently spends a lot of free time, and the campaign for a commutation of her sentence made much of this conversion. She was an entirely different person now, her advocates stressed; kill her and you'd be killing someone other than the woman who'd committed the murders.

The other side pointed out that, even if the conversion was genuine, it had only come about because Karla Faye had a date with the needle. Yes, she'd earned herself a place in Heaven. No, she couldn't postpone the trip. Your bus is waitin', Karla Faye!

What brought the case to Doak's mind had nothing to do with arguments for and against capital punishment, an issue on which his views tended to shift anyway. But he remembered something someone had said right around the time that *60 Minutes* was airing the woman's story, and George W. Bush, still in the Governor's Mansion in Austin, was turning down her appeal:

"If she wasn't pretty, nobody'd give a damn."

Well, somebody would. The die-hard opponents of capital punishment would be on board no matter who she was or what she looked like. But if she'd had a face like a pizza, there'd have been fewer signatures on those petitions, fewer feet marching, and a lot less face time on network television.

But she was a pretty woman, maybe even beautiful. That got her more attention, got her special treatment.

So he was thinking about the woman he was going to meet tomorrow. Lisa Yarrow Otterbein, who was better looking than Karla Faye Tucker, and who, as far as he knew, had never even laid hands on a pickax.

The Wikipedia page showed a photo of Karla Faye Tucker, and he pulled up Lisa's photo on his phone and held it alongside of Karla Faye's for comparison.

No comparison, really.

Radburn's photo was a good one, he noted. Except that it was static, a single moment frozen in time, and she had one of those faces that kept changing, looking slightly different from every different angle, changing too as whatever was going through her mind played itself out on her face.

A man could spend a lifetime looking at a face like that.

Jesus, he thought.

He opened MS Word, clicked to open a new document. His fingers hovered over the keyboard, and then he changed his mind, just as he'd changed his mind about the credit card. He closed Word, then shut down his computer altogether.

Found a tablet. The old-fashioned kind, a yellow legal pad, ruled sheets of paper 8-1/2 by 11 inches. Uncapped a Bic ballpoint, began printing in block capitals.

He was at his desk for the better part of an hour. There were plenty of pauses, a lot of gazing off into the middle distance, chasing the thoughts that flitted across the surface of his consciousness. And from time to time he'd pick up his phone and find his way to her photograph.

A good photo, but there was so much it couldn't show. Including the color of her eyes.

They were blue.

He set the alarm for eight and woke at seven-thirty as if from a dream. But there were no dream memories, no clue to the dream's theme or subject.

He showered, dressed. He'd laid out clothes before he went to bed, and they were on the chair waiting for him—boxer shorts, dark trousers, a long-sleeved shirt with a tropical print. A parrot, a palm tree, just the sort of thing a snowbird would buy the day after he got off the plane.

He'd bought it himself in a strip mall halfway between Tampa and Perry. Hardly ever wore it since.

Along with the clothes, the chair held the recording device the sheriff had reminded him not to forget. He fastened the rig around his chest, clicked it on and off and on again, said "Testing, one two three," which was what everyone said under the circumstances, probably because it was easier than thinking of something else to say. He played it back, heard the words in his own voice.

It always surprised him, hearing his own voice. It was never the way he thought he sounded.

The shirt covered the wire. Nothing showed. He slipped his hand between two shirt buttons, switched the thing on, played the test again, then erased it. He said, "Recorded in the parking lot of the Winn-Dixie supermarket on Cable Boulevard in Belle Vista, Gallatin County, Florida, this sixteenth day of April in the year two thousand fourteen. Participants are J. W. Miller and Lisa Yarrow Otterbein."

Stopped it, played it back. He'd spoken in his everyday voice, but how much of that was New York and how much had turned Floridian was hard for him to tell. He'd speak differently as Frankie from Bergen County, and he wouldn't have to think about the accent. All he had to do was get the attitude right and the accent would follow.

He checked his wristwatch for the tenth or twentieth time. The time raced or crawled, it was hard to say which. He didn't want to do this, and at the same time he wanted to do it and be done with it.

✿

He circled the Winn-Dixie lot a few minutes before eleven, looked for a silver-gray Lexus, looked for any car parked off by itself.

Nothing. He drove a few blocks away and parked on the street. Checked the wire, made sure it was still working. Picked up the yellow pad, looked it over, shook his head at what he'd written.

Took out his phone, checked to see if anyone had called. He'd switched it from Ring to Vibrate before he left the house, because he didn't want to get a phone call while he was busy being Frankie from Jersey.

No calls.

He summoned up her photo. Surprising, really, that you couldn't determine the color of her eyes. They were such a vivid blue you'd think the camera couldn't help picking it up.

He put the phone away. Checked his watch again, and returned to the Winn-Dixie. The parking spot he picked was at the rear of the lot and over to the left. There were no other cars within thirty yards of it.

He was ten minutes early, which was about right. He should be here first. Let her come to him.

If she did.

He hadn't really entertained the possibility that she'd fail to show, but now it seemed highly probable. It was, after all, one thing to broach the subject to someone you knew, even as superficially as she knew Gonson. It was another thing to meet with a complete stranger and pay him a down payment on a contract killing.

She'd skip the meeting, he decided. She'd stay home and give it some more thought, and then she'd tell Richard Lyle Gonson that she'd changed her mind. Or she'd make up a story explaining why she'd been unable to get to the Winn-Dixie lot at the appointed hour, and looking to reschedule. And there'd be more phone calls all around, and tomorrow morning or the day after he'd be sitting where he was sitting now, only this time she'd show up, because she wouldn't pull the same crap twice. And—

And there she was. A silver sedan, but was it a Lexus? Cars tended to look alike these days—although nothing out there looked much like his Monte Carlo. But this was indeed a Lexus, he recognized the hood emblem, and it was skirting the several rows of cars huddled around the store entrance and heading instead for the rear of the lot.

She seemed to hesitate, settling at length on a spot one row in front of him and four spaces off to the left. She shut off the ignition, stayed behind the wheel.

Did she want a sign? All right, he could give her one. He flicked his headlights on and off, then on and off again. Was that entrapment? He decided it wasn't, not unless she was a moth.

Her door opened and she got out of the car. She was wearing a burnt orange top over a pair of powder-blue designer jeans. A tan leather bag rode her shoulder, and one hand pinned it to her side, as if to secure the thousand dollars.

He leaned across the passenger seat, opened the door for her. She hesitated for a beat, and he patted the seat in invitation. She got in and drew the door shut.